Secrets...
& Confessions

...*Plus!*

ARE YOU A BEACH BABE?
TRY OUR FAB QUIZ AT THE
BACK OF THE BOOK

SOME SECRETS ARE JUST TOO GOOD TO KEEP TO YOURSELF!

Sugar Secrets...

Sugar
SECRETS...

...& Confessions

Mel Sparke

An imprint of HarperCollins*Publishers*

Published in Great Britain by Collins in 2000
Collins is an imprint of HarperCollins*Publishers* Ltd
77–85 Fulham Palace Road, Hammersmith, London W6 8JB

The HarperCollins website address is
www.**fire**and**water**.com

9 8 7 6 5 4 3 2 1

Creative consultant: Sue Dando
Copyright © Sugar 2000. Licensed with TLC.

ISBN 0 00 710198 8

Printed and bound in Great Britain by
Omnia Books Limited, Glasgow

Conditions of Sale

CHAPTER 1

• •

THE PHONE CALL

Ollie Stanton turned off the coffee machine for the day and found his gaze drawn to the bright sunshine outside the End-of-the-Line café. It was a warm Sunday afternoon out there, the sort that made him glad to be a part of life and everything that happened in it. It was, Ollie suddenly decided, the kind of day for doing something daft and not giving a damn if anyone saw.

He started humming the tune to The Loud's *Waiting for the Day*. Taking his blue and white J cloth, he began wiping down the chrome on the coffee machine, while bobbing up and down to the rhythm of the song. In his head The Loud was playing to a packed Wembley Stadium and Ollie was strutting across the vast stage in four grand's worth of Gaultier combats and jacket, the power of his voice reverberating around the vast arena.

"*Waiting for the day, when you will be there...*"
Ollie turned and sang to his friends, who were
lounging in their usual spot by the window, then
took hold of a stainless steel sandwich platter
from under the counter and began playing it like a
guitar.

Joe Gladwin turned, laughed and decided to
join in, using the table as a makeshift drum kit,
and tapping his hands on it in time to Ollie's
vocals.

Others began singing, taking the little packets
of sugar from the bowl and shaking them up and
down, or banging nearby surfaces with cutlery or
Coke cans in time to the tune they all knew off by
heart.

Soon Ollie was standing on a chair, gyrating
his hips, his makeshift guitar held high above his
head. As far as he was concerned, he *was* a rock
star.

Kerry Bellamy grinned at her boyfriend and
gave him the thumbs up. "Nice one, Ol," she
laughed. "Just what we need to wind down after
the last few weeks of hell." She turned and
nudged Sonja Harvey, urging her to join in with
everyone else.

Sonja looked up from the magazine she'd been
staring at and gave Kerry a half-hearted smile.

Then she looked down at her magazine again, lost in her own thoughts.

She's probably as knackered as me from all that studying, Kerry figured and felt a wave of relief wash over her at the thought of having no more A level exams to worry about.

Anna Michaels wandered out from the kitchen to see what all the noise was about. Tensing slightly when she saw Ollie giving it loads from a chair, she quickly relaxed again when she scanned the café and realised only her friends were left.

"It's a good job we're about to close," she teased, her Marigolds covered in soap bubbles, "or you'd have cleared the place of customers by now! I could do with you lot on a Friday night when I want to get off home early. What's the occasion?"

Ollie turned and gave an exaggerated shrug. "No reason, I guess," he shouted, breaking off from strumming his platter. "Just having a good time, you know..."

"Helping us forget the strain of the last few weeks," shouted Kerry above the din.

"Yeah," Joe agreed. "Getting us in the mood for a long, scorching summer."

"Or a wet, windy one," said Matt Ryan, deadpan.

Kerry sighed. "These exams have been the

worst yet... like you'd expect from your A levels, I guess..." she added unnecessarily. She pushed her glasses further up her nose and giggled.

Kerry knew she was stating the obvious – what with her, Joe and Sonja frantically cramming as much revision as possible into their lives recently, there hadn't been much chance for them to let off steam. Now though, the only thing that Kerry had to think about was what she was going to wear each morning. That and her upcoming holiday to Ibiza with Ollie, the thought of which made her stomach lurch in a mixture of excitement and anticipation.

As Anna retreated to the kitchen to finish clearing up, she heard the faint sound of the telephone ringing above the noise. Turning back, she picked up the wall phone by the jukebox and stuffed her rubber-gloved hand over her ear, screwing her face up to hear what the person at the end of the line was saying.

"Ol, it's for you!" she shouted at the top of her voice, waving the phone at him.

Ollie leapt off his chair like a gazelle and bounded over to the phone, which he smilingly took from Anna.

"Hell-*lo*..." he said chirpily and began doing a silly dance in front of his friends who had just noisily started on the chorus to *Waiting*... Then, as he listened to the voice at the other end of the line, Ollie suddenly stopped jigging around and the grin on his face turned to a look of astonishment. He motioned to the others to be quiet then stuck the index finger of his free hand into his ear and frowned. Everyone shut up and strained to hear his end of the conversation, listening for clues as to what the sudden seriousness was about.

"Uh... yep," they heard him say. "Oh. *Really*? ... You're kidding me, right?" Ollie ran his free hand through his already ruffled hair and looked boggle-eyed at his friends.

"*Really*?" he said again, only this time half an octave higher. "Yeah, of course we would! ... I can't believe it. Are you sure this isn't a wind-up? Yeah? Wow, that's great! Uh... I'll wait to hear from you then. Right. And, um, thanks for calling."

Ollie placed the phone back on its cradle, punched the air and gave an almighty whoop. "You'll never guess what..." he yelped, leaping the few strides back to the gang's table in one, and clutching his head in shock.

Everyone looked at him expectantly.

"Come on, then," Matt demanded impatiently. "You gonna tell us, or what?"

"That was..." Ollie stopped for a moment and

gulped. "It was only one of the promoters of the Dansby Music Festival!"

Several heads nodded in recognition. Everyone in the gang knew about the event which was happening in a couple of weeks' time. They'd spoken about it loads of times recently, gossiping about the big name acts that were headlining over the two days, or reading snippets out of the newspapers.

"Yeah. So...?" prompted Matt.

"Right, er... so, *well*," Ollie carried on, stumbling over the words in his excitement, "this Saul guy heard us at the Battle of the Bands competition and... and, anyway, that was him on the phone and he only wants to book us for the festival. Can you believe it?!"

Wide-eyed and flushed with anticipation, Ollie grabbed Joe by the shoulders and dragged him out of his seat. Exchanging a euphoric high-five, the pair of them began singing again, dancing round and round the café until the song deteriorated into laughing and whooping. They began bumping into tables and chairs, but they didn't care because they felt as if they'd just won the Lottery.

"Ol, that's amazing news!" beamed Matt, leaping up to join them. "Wow, this could finally be your big break."

Ollie checked himself for a moment and shook his head. "I tell you, Matt, I'm excited, but I'm gonna be a whole lot more realistic about this than I was about the Battle of the Bands competition. I mean, I thought we were going places when we got through to the final of that and look what happened then – the whole thing was a fix. Believe me, I'm gonna try and be a bit more grounded about this…"

"So how come you've got a grin a mile wide on your face, buddy boy?" Matt joked, punching his friend gently in the ribs. "Anyway, if it hadn't been for that competition, you would never have got this phone call, right? And for all you know, this might lead on to a record deal."

"Oh, God, please don't say that, Matt," Ollie cut in, his eyes wide. "You're getting me all goosebumpy just at the thought of it."

"So much for not getting too excited," laughed Kerry.

"Can you imagine," Catrina Osgood broke in, "before you know it, you might be on *Top of the Pops*. Can I do your make-up when it happens? Go on, Ol, *pleeease*."

"And I could be your official photographer," Maya Joshi joined in, warming to the fantasy. "There to do your album covers, publicity shots…"

"Hey, you lot, steady on!" Andy King, The Loud's bassist, chuckled, the hairs on his neck standing on end at the very thought. "Let's take it one step at a time, shall we?"

"No, mate," interrupted Matt. "Let's celebrate! Hey, Anna – Cokes and crisps all round. Ollie's treat."

"If I'm paying, it's just *one* Coke and *one* packet of salt and vinegar to share, OK?" Ollie joked, ruffling Matt's hair. Everyone in the café laughed.

Everyone except Sonja. She didn't join in with the fun. Sure, she'd smiled at Ollie's news, she'd patted Joe on the back and said, "Well done." But now she was doing what she had been for most of the afternoon: staring out of the window or at her magazine, with a faraway look on her face.

CHAPTER 2

● ●

MATT'S BRILLIANT IDEA

I can't believe how I've messed up, Sonja thought angrily. *Everyone else is having a fabulous time because it's the end of exams and I should be too. As it is, I've got nothing to celebrate.* She stared at the unread magazine in front of her and wished she was anywhere but in the café right now.

Sonja suddenly felt stupid for coming to her usual haunt with the others. She had thought it might lift her spirits a bit, maybe take her mind off her problem. But now she was here, and because it was obvious that everyone else was in such a good mood, she wished she had stayed at home. In her room. Alone.

For the first time in her life Sonja felt she was drowning and it was a sensation that was completely alien to her. She had always been so sure about the path her life was going to take. Get good grades throughout school, go to university, get a First in Public Relations, get a good job with a flat and a nice car, have a career, a good time, loads of money, and a fab boyfriend (preferably Owen)...

The plan in her head had never deviated far from that – there was never anything else to consider, like flunking school or deciding to go off travelling, the sort of stuff that a lot of other people her age did.

Now, everything was different. The only certainty was that her plans were falling apart right before her eyes. She felt helpless to do anything to stop it. And doubly angry because of that.

"Hey, Son, why the long face?"

Matt interrupted Sonja's brooding with a friendly kiss on the cheek and his most winning smile. Moments ago he had been dancing around the tables with the boys, singing cheerfully at the top of his voice. Then he'd spotted Sonja sort of smiling and joining in, but obviously miles away. She looked distracted and he figured he was just the person to make her snap out of it.

"Uh, nothing to worry about, Matt, I'm just a bit tired, that's all." Sonja found herself fiddling nervously with her magazine as she spoke, flicking through the pages without actually taking in what was on them.

"Great news about the band, isn't it?" he grinned, sliding into the seat beside her and putting an arm round her shoulder.

Sonja had a vague idea what he was talking about, though she hadn't listened to much of the conversation that had gone on earlier. "Er, yeah, fabulous," she said as lightly as possible. "Nice one."

"And I bet you're glad your exams are over now, aren't you?" continued Matt cheerfully. "It must be quite a relief not to have to wake up every morning worrying about what exam you've got or how well you did in the last one. Not that you ever let them get on top of you – you're far too cool for that..."

If only you knew, Sonja thought bitterly.

"Hey, I've just had an idea," said Matt suddenly, speaking to the rest of the group, and waving his arms up and down in an attempt to get everyone to shut up.

"Hold the front page, guys, Matt's having a thought!" Ollie shouted. "This is like the Millennium – it won't happen again for another thousand years."

"Ha *ha.* As I was saying... why don't we all pile down to the festival and make a weekend of it? We could take a tent – my old man's got one in the garage somewhere – load up with sleeping bags… It'd be a right laugh. What d'you think?"

"Matt, that's about the best idea you've ever had," said Ollie in mock astonishment.

"It's the *only* idea he's ever had," quipped Cat.

"It is – though I love it, it's brilliant." Ollie was really animated now. He leapt up and down, his arms waving around like windmills. "We've got a massive tent somewhere at home too. I'm sure that between the two of them we could all squeeze in. We could pile into a couple of cars, drive down and make a big party of it. It'll be great – a fantastic weekend away!"

"You're not working that weekend then, Ol?" Kerry prompted gently, keen to make sure Ollie didn't get carried away only to find he had a shift or two at the End. After the animosity the recent Battle of the Bands competition had caused, with Ollie expecting time off work that wasn't his to take, she didn't want her boyfriend getting into trouble with his Uncle Nick or upsetting Anna again.

"I don't even need to look," Ollie said confidently. "I've got that weekend off. I booked it ages ago because there's a two-day bike fair in the city. I was going to go and get some parts for the Vespa. Not any more though. This has got to be a much better offer."

"What about you, Anna?" asked Kerry. "Are you working?"

Anna went and peered at the work rota hanging on the wall.

"I am on the Saturday," she called, "and Nick's down for Sunday. I could catch a train late on Saturday afternoon if someone could pick me up from the nearest station."

"No worries, I will. So are we all on then?" Matt demanded, slapping his hands on the Formica tabletop and looking expectantly around him.

"Do they have electricity at these places?" Cat piped up innocently. "Only I'd need to take a hairdryer with me. And my skin purifier. And there'd be somewhere I could have a shower, wouldn't there?"

She looked blankly at the sea of faces who were now in various states of suppressed hysterics.

"Cat, it's not like a hotel," Matt explained through a mouthful of giggles. "Heck – I doubt if it'll even be like a proper camp site. You'll be lucky if you get a saucepan of lukewarm water to wash in, let alone anything so fancy as a shower. Or if there is, it'll be a cold one, in the open air, that you'll be sharing with several hundred others."

"Sounds perfectly hideous," replied Cat, curling her lip distastefully. "I suppose I'll just have to make sure I don't get dirty then. And I suppose I could tie my hair back and wear my oldest clothes and espadrilles..."

"Let's pray it doesn't rain," Ollie smirked, his mind wandering to the mud-engulfed music festivals he'd been to in the past, "or you'll be wanting to come home as soon as you get there. What about you, Kez? D'you think you can square it with your parents and your Saturday job?"

"I should think so, as long as I butter Mum and Dad up between now and then. And I've got a few weekdays lined up at the chemist over the summer, so I expect I can sort it so that I change a Saturday for one of those. How about you, Son?"

Sonja didn't answer. She was staring blankly at the back wall of the café. Matt poked her in the arm, making her jump.

"Wh-what?" she said, her eyes scanning the group who were all watching her. "Uh. yeah, sure, whatever," she replied, shuffling edgily in her seat.

"Well, I hope you guys have a great time. Send me a postcard, won't you?" Maya suddenly announced from the corner where she'd been sitting quietly.

"Oh, yes, *of course*," said Kerry, shooting a

sympathetic look at Maya. "Your parents are going to love this one, aren't they?"

"Uh-huh." The tone was rueful. "There's no way they're going to let me go camping in a field in the middle of nowhere with several thousand ravers, are they? I mean, come on, they're doctors – and ones with overactive imaginations at that. As far as they're concerned, the place'll be crawling with drug pushers and rapists, desperate to get me hooked on something or attack me in my tent. They'll never let me go. Not in a million years..."

CHAPTER 3

●●●●●●●●●●●●●●●●●●●●●●●●●●●●●

MOVING ON

"Are we ready then?"

Joe pulled open the driver's door of his car, slid into the seat and waited for Ollie to climb in next to him. Having only recently passed his test, he still hadn't quite got used to having a friend in the car with him, rather than his driving instructor or his dad. And it was weird not having someone telling him what to do, where to turn, pull in or overtake.

But he loved his car. It gave him the freedom he needed and would be perfect for bombing up and down between Winstead and London when he went to university in October. *Assuming I get the grades*, Joe kept telling himself.

And of course, it'd have to get him to Brighton and back more than anywhere, so he could see his girlfriend, Meg, who was going to be studying there. His heart turned cartwheels at the thought of her. Joe's life had taken on a whole new meaning since he'd met her at his father's wedding a few weeks ago. He felt there was a new purpose to living.

He wondered how Meg was getting on with her parents on holiday in Greece. Before she'd met Joe she'd been really looking forward to getting away once her exams were over, but now... now she just wished he was going too. Joe thought that was sweet when she'd told him. Still, at least she'd be back at home on Saturday. Then he could tell her his news about the festival and invite her along. It'd be the perfect excuse to spend a lot more time with her.

Ollie interrupted Joe's romantic thoughts and brought him back to the present.

"You know, it's hard to keep level-headed about this festival thing," he said, turning to Joe with anticipation written all over his face. "I mean, I know we're only one of maybe seven or eight unknown bands playing, but even so, it's such a massive opportunity. There are bound to be loads of people in the music business there – A and R, independent labels, other promoters. If something doesn't come out of it then maybe we don't *deserve* to make it!" Ollie thumped the dashboard so hard it made Joe's battered Fiat rattle alarmingly.

"Steady on, mate, one false move and it's likely to fall apart," joked Joe, patting the steering wheel in front of him as he slotted his key into the ignition.

"Sorry," Ollie chuckled. "I'm just getting a bit wound up, that's all. Anyway, you know what I mean, don't you? About the band?"

"Oh, sure. I feel exactly the same way," said Joe, starting the engine and putting his seat belt on. "I only wish I was gonna be around more once summer's over. I tell you what, it'll be just my luck if the band takes off once I've upped and left for London. There you'll be, giving it loads on MTV, with another drummer – one who can make rehearsals at the drop of a hat. And I'll be relegated to watching you on the telly from my grotty hall of residence, forever doomed to be known as the saddo who got left behind."

"Aw, don't worry, mate," chuckled Ollie. "We might send you a postcard from the video shoot in the Caribbean: y'know, 'Look what you're missing out on. Loser!' Or something. We'll even fax you a copy of our first cheque when we sign to a major record company... '£400,000 – read it and weep. Love, your old mate, Ollie Stanton.'"

"And when you're playing Wembley I'll be

phoning you up, begging to be put on the guest list, and you'll refuse to take my calls."

"As if I'd do a rotten thing like that," Ollie protested, grinning manically at the thought.

They drove towards Central Sounds where they were meeting Matt to look for some better equipment to hire for the festival. Joe found himself thinking back to the moment at the end of the Battle of the Bands competition when he'd told Ollie – in no uncertain terms – that by September he wouldn't be involved in The Loud any more. *He* was going off to London and *stuff you*, Ollie (or at least, that's how it had come across).

At the time Joe had been angry with the way Ollie had been riding roughshod over his friends (in particular Anna) to further The Loud's cause.

Later, when they'd both had time to calm down, it was Ollie who had made peace between them. It had been on the Sunday in the café after Ollie had made amends with Anna. He'd presented her with the beauty voucher The Loud had won as their prize for being runners-up in the competition. Afterwards, Ollie had walked over to Joe and apologised "for being a prat".

"Oh, right," Joe had said. "It's OK. Actually, I was going to say sorry to you too."

"For...?"

"For telling you I was leaving the band in the way that I did."

"What, you mean shouting 'I'm leaving the band!' at me after the competition, then us not speaking the whole way home in the minibus?" Ollie had giggled and soon the two friends were joking about the incident, all animosity between them forgotten.

Joe found himself chuckling out loud as he drove along the high street towards the music shop.

"What's so funny?" asked Ollie.

"I was just thinking about us falling out after the competition. It was weird not speaking to you. But I guess one big row in all the years we've known each other is pretty good going."

"You're right. But then if we fell out much more than that, we wouldn't have stayed mates, would we? Or be playing together in a band?"

"Even if it's not for much longer," Joe said woefully.

"Actually, I've been thinking about what you said that day about not being in the band any more, and so long as you keep churning out songs for us, and making the trips home, I think we can work something out," said Ollie cheerily.

"Well, of course there's Meg now, but I'm bound to be coming home quite often, if only so that Mum can do my washing," Joe laughed. "And as for the songwriting – well, it doesn't matter where I live, I'll always write. I can't imagine not doing it. I'm writing something new right now – d'you want me to get it done for the festival?"

"Yeah? What's it like?" Ollie demanded excitedly.

"Well, it's a bit of a love song actually," said Joe, blushing. "It's something I'm writing for Meg."

"Oh wow, man, that's great!" Ollie enthused. "And it'll be ready for us to rehearse before Dansby?"

Joe nodded. "I think so."

"Well, that's settled then. There's no *way* you're leaving the band. I know you'll be in London and won't be around much, but when you're not studying – or snogging Meg – you can come home, dump your laundry, pick up your sticks and carry on where you left off."

Joe frowned. "But what'll you do the rest of the time, when you've got a gig and I can't make it?"

"It'll be all right," Ollie replied airily. "We'll have to call in a sub. Get in a session musician. Don't worry, we'll work something out so everyone's happy. Just make sure you don't go off and join a band down there."

"Now there's a thought," hooted Joe. "I could go and get myself involved in next year's Travis. Then *I'll* be the one coming back and wafting my wads around, rubbing your noses in it."

"Don't even try it, mate, or you'll have me to answer to."

CHAPTER 4

• •

LISTENING IN

"Brrrrr...brrrrr...brrrrr..."

Ollie turned away from the chip fryer he'd just switched on and leapt in the direction of the ringing phone.

"I'll get it," he shouted as he hurried through the kitchen, past Nick and Anna, who were going through the café order book trying to work out why they'd had a delivery of fifty bagels instead of fifteen that morning.

"I still don't understand how you didn't notice when they arrived," Ollie heard Nick saying to Anna as he rushed for the phone in the café.

"They were hidden under umpteen sliced whites and crusty cobs, that's why," replied Anna. "I didn't see them until the baker had gone."

Ollie picked up the receiver. *Please let it be Saul*, he prayed to himself, crossing his fingers for luck. But it was soon obvious it wasn't the Dansby promoter he was so desperate to hear from. Judging by the time delay, the call sounded as if it was from abroad.

"Hello. May I speak with Nichol*aaas*?" the American-sounding woman drawled.

"Sorry? Who?" Ollie asked, his brow furrowed.

"Nichol*aaas* Stanton. Perhaps I've dialled the wrong number...?"

The penny dropped. "Oh, you mean *Nick?*" Ollie exclaimed. "I got confused there for a minute. Hold on. I'll get him for you."

Dammit! Ollie cursed.

It was two days since the unexpected call from that Saul guy. He hadn't left a contact number, just said he'd be in touch. Although Ollie figured he must be busy working on such a big event, he'd hoped to have heard from Saul again by now. In bleaker moments Ollie wondered if it wasn't just someone messing around. *Yeah, great joke if it is*, Ollie thought bitterly. *Like I'm really laughing*.

"For you, Nick," Ollie yelled, dropping the phone on to the table in front of him and heading despondently back to his fryer to throw in a pile of uncooked chips.

Nick carried on rifling through the reams of delivery notes in front of him, talking intently to Anna. He either hadn't heard or was ignoring Ollie.

"Hey, Nicho*laaas*!" Ollie persisted, when he realised his uncle had made no move towards the telephone. "There's a woman on the phone for you – sounds like she's calling from America."

Nick's head jerked round to look at Ollie. His mouth fell open.

"Seriously?" he demanded, clearly shocked.

"Uh-huh. Well, she had an American accent and there's a time delay on the line."

Nick hotfooted it through the kitchen, into the café and grabbed the receiver. Putting his hand over the mouthpiece, he looked behind him to see if Anna and Ollie were listening in. Which of course they were, both having followed him to stare.

"We'll be getting busy soon," he hissed. "Can we have some action in there or something?"

Anna and Ollie looked at each other from behind the café counter and smiled.

"I *was* pretty busy, thanks, until you had a paddy over the bread order," Anna hissed back, playfully flicking a hand towel in his direction and heading back into the kitchen.

"Keep an eye on the chips, Anna," said Ollie

as he picked up a damp cloth and sauntered over to a table to begin wiping it down. He was keen to hear who it was that had flustered his uncle so much. But Nick kept his hand over the receiver and looked pointedly at his nephew, who, on spying a group of people coming into the café, admitted defeat and left him in peace.

As he took orders, Ollie tried to keep one ear on the conversation going on between his uncle and the mystery lady. She seemed to be doing most of the talking, while Nick roared with over-the-top laughter every now and again or came out with what sounded to Ollie like corny old chat-up lines.

This made Ollie cringe and he'd catch Anna's eye then stick his fingers down his throat, pretending to be sick, which made her laugh out loud.

When the long exchange came to an end, Ollie couldn't wait to try and wind his uncle up.

"So, who was that on the phone?" he asked innocently. "Someone putting in a sandwich order from America?"

Nick blustered his way past Ollie, determined not to rise to the bait.

"Just someone I met in Nashville," he said, adding, "have you done that order of fries yet?"

"Yep. She seemed *very* friendly," Ollie pressed.

"May I speak with Nicho*laaaaas* please?'" he imitated, exaggerating her accent. "Get to know her well out there?"

"Don't be daft," answered Nick. "We just happened to like the same music and she promised to try and get some records for me out there. She was calling to let me know she'd found them. Now, is that it or is there anything else you want to know?"

Ollie and Anna giggled at the look on Nick's face and carried on with their duties, enjoying seeing the normally laid-back Nick getting somewhat riled by Ollie's teasing.

The café bell went and a load of noisy lads came in. Ollie turned to see Matt, Joe, Andy and another guy he didn't recognise, heading towards the crowd's usual table.

"Hi, Ol," called Matt, throwing a menu at the new guy. "A massive fry-up for me and whatever this lot are having, please. We bumped into each other at Central Sounds. I was window shopping, like you do when you're skint..."

"And me and Andy were fantasising about what we'd buy there if we had endless pots of money," Joe added.

"Yeah, we could have kitted ourselves out like Oasis if we had the odd ten grand to spare."

"But then all the money in the world wouldn't

31

make Ollie a better singer, would it?" teased Matt, his face cracking into a wide grin.

"No, and the more stuff we hire, the more chance it gives our sound engineer to make a balls-up, doesn't it?" Ollie retorted, laughing at Matt.

"We met my old mate Deke there too," Matt carried on. The guy sitting next to Matt nodded to Ollie then carried on studying his menu. "We used to be at school together, then he left and picked up this brilliant job working for a big music promoter, which involves him swanning around the country putting on acts at different venues and earning pots of money. While I, on the other hand, left school and bummed around and did nothing. Story of my life, eh?"

"Someone pass the man a tissue," suggested Andy.

"Anyway," continued Matt, idly scratching his head, "window shopping like that gave me some ideas for my music system at home. I reckon that I could take in a load of my old equipment and trade it in for a few bits of new stuff. Then, for my next party, I could have the sound so fantastic everyone'll think they're up the front of a Chemical Brothers gig at Brixton Academy."

Deke laughed.

"No, seriously, it's gonna be my biggest and

best party yet. One you'll all be talking about for months."

Now it was Andy's turn to laugh. "What, you mean more of a talking point than the one where your house nearly got burnt down?"

"Uh, well, I guess that was notorious for all the wrong reasons," Matt replied. "This one'll be cracking though, I promise you."

"Hey, Matt, it sounds like you have some, er, *interesting* parties," smirked Deke.

"I do. Why don't you come to the next one?"

"I thought you'd never ask. So when is it and where?"

"Saturday night. Eight till late. Be there or... don't."

"Nice one, mate."

A shriek of laughter from the table in the corner made them glance round briefly. No one had noticed Maya's thirteen-year-old sister, Sunny Joshi, arrive with her friends. The sight of two older lads looking at their table made the younger girls burst into further explosive giggles.

"That new boy's fit," Sunny remarked in a low voice to her mate, Lucy. "I wouldn't mind swapping saliva with *him*."

Lucy glanced over to take a look at Deke. "He's OK, but I still prefer that Matt guy. He's just to die for."

"Nah, too girlie-looking for me," Sunny whispered. "I prefer 'em a bit more macho and rough around the edges."

Her girlfriends tittered into their drinks. Then, as they saw Deke stand up, they nudged each other and all turned to stare at him.

Deke smiled smugly at the effect he was having on them, then turned back to the others. "I've got to shoot," he said, making his way to the door. "I'll see you guys later."

"Yeah, sure, Deke," Matt said in a loud voice. "Don't forget the party on Saturday."

"I'll be there."

"Now's your chance," Sunny's friend Marsha hissed to her. "I dare you to follow him and chat him up!"

Sunny thought for a moment before replying. "Nah, not here. But I know how we could get to know them all a lot better..."

CHAPTER 5

● ●

SONJA'S GROWING PROBLEM

Sonja chucked her bag on the floor just inside the front door and wandered through to the lounge, then into the kitchen. The house seemed deserted, as it had been when she'd first left fifteen minutes ago. Sonja was relieved. She filled the kettle with water, scooped a spoonful of instant coffee into a mug, then absent-mindedly wandered off, back into the lounge, where she picked up the remote control and flicked on the TV.

She then headed into the hall, picked up her bag, took it through to the kitchen and dumped it on to the scrubbed pine table. She began rooting through it, looking for what she'd just walked to the newsagent's for. Then Sonja remembered. She hadn't bought anything. She knew she'd gone there for something, but once she'd got inside, her mind had gone AWOL. A bit like it was now, and much as it had been for some time.

Sonja drifted back into the lounge, flicked through the TV channels, returned to the kitchen and poured water from the kettle into her mug. Slopping in the milk and stirring it with a spoon, she wandered back to the lounge and slumped on to the enormous padded sofa. Staring at the television but not taking in the programme, she took a sip of coffee and grimaced. It was cold. *Yuk!* She must have forgotten to turn the kettle on.

Sonja felt like screaming with exasperation and not for the first time in recent days; she hated being out of control like this. The irritation turned to annoyance when she heard the telephone start to ring, and by the fifth ring realised the answering machine wasn't on. Sonja really didn't feel like talking to anyone, but she couldn't just ignore it.

Banging her mug carelessly on to the coffee table and tutting as its contents spilled all over the glass top, she heaved herself off the sofa and went to the phone.

"Hello..." she said glumly.

"Hiya, Son, it's me."

Sonja was so shocked to hear Owen Michael's

voice she nearly dropped the phone. Which was crazy, seeing as it wasn't at all unusual for her boyfriend to call up like this. It was just that now – *now* – everything was different.

"Hel-*lo*, Son? Are you still there?"

Sonja gathered herself together and finally answered. "Hi, Owen. Sorry, I... er, was watching the telly. Hang on a minute, I'll turn it off."

She put the phone down and dragged herself over to the television, buying time by walking as slowly as possible, her mind racing. *What shall I tell him? Should I get it over with right now? Or not?* Sonja came back and picked up the phone again.

"That's better," she said, "I can hear you now."

"Not disturbing your soapfest, am I?" Owen joked. "I can call back if the *Neighbours* are in some kind of crisis. Or if Sally from *Home and Away* has just had a bust up with Alf. I don't want to ruin your teatime viewing."

Sonja smiled for the first time in days. Trust Owen to take the mick. He knew she liked to watch the soaps, following the lives of, as he called it, "fictitious weirdos on the other side of the world."

"It's OK," she said. "Anyway, what are you doing calling me at this time? Aren't you at work?"

"Well, actually, I *am* at work, but I had to tell you. I've got some great news..."

Glad someone has, thought Sonja. "Go on then..." she prompted.

"I'm coming to the city. Next week, for a training course. I'm being put up in a swanky hotel on Monday and Tuesday, so I thought I'd come down a day earlier and stay with Anna on Sunday night. I've already spoken to her and she's cool about it. So I thought we could get together on Sunday evening. That is, if you want to."

Sonja was stunned. *This is a sign...* she thought. *For me to tell him face to face. Yeah,* she reassured herself, *far better to tell him like that than over the phone. At least then I can gauge his reaction a bit better.*

"That's great," she replied. "Really good news."

"Are you *sure*?" Owen asked, a little perplexed. By his reckoning, she didn't sound too enthusiastic about the idea. "I mean, if you've already got something planned..."

"No, nothing planned. Honest. It'll be fun..."

"So, I'll call you nearer the time to arrange to meet up, OK?"

"Great. Uh... look, there's someone at the door," Sonja lied. "I've got to go. I'll see you on Sunday, all right?"

"Yeah, bye then."

Owen put down the receiver and sat staring at it for a few moments. Something was up, but he had no idea what.

Sonja, meanwhile, came off the phone and began silently weeping tears of fear and relief all rolled into one.

At last I'm going to be able to talk about this, she thought, *because I don't know if I can cope on my own for much longer. It's good that I'll be seeing Owen in a few days time. At least then I can tell him.*

She looked down at her stomach and began prodding at the flesh of her bare belly which was exposed between pink hipsters and a white cropped top.

Won't be able to wear these for much longer, she thought. *I wonder when it will start to show?* With a tummy as flat as hers, it wouldn't be long, of that she was sure. Even if she wanted to keep the news to herself – and Owen – it would soon be obvious to anyone who cared to look that Sonja was pregnant.

CHAPTER 6

●●●●●●●●●●●●●●●●●●●●●●●●●●●●

DOUBLE STANDARDS

"Go on, you have to do it..."

"You'll never know unless you ask."

"Chicken out now and it'll just keep on bugging you and bugging you. You might as well get it over and done with."

"Come on, Maya, just do it. For our sakes if no one else's. You've been going around with a mouth like a dead fish ever since we decided to go to the festival."

Maya sat on the wall outside her house and laughed.

"Cheers, Ol, you're all heart." She turned to Kerry and Joe and smiled. "I know you're all absolutely right. It's just that I reckon I've got about as much chance of my parents letting me go to the festival as I have of them letting me drop out of school to run aromatherapy classes for rugby players. Basically, it's a complete non-starter."

"Hey, they might surprise you," Kerry reassured her. "Look how they were about Alex."

Maya wasn't convinced. "Hmmm, but that was only after they'd met him and realised what a responsible human being he was. Before that the thought of me going out with any guy, let alone one so much older than me, made them flip. They'll be just the same about this."

"I'll tell you what," Ollie said. "Why don't you go into your house, put it to your parents, and we'll all sit on this wall and stay here until you come back out and tell us what happened."

Ollie grinned then added, "No pressure!"

Maya rolled her eyes. "You're welcome to stay on my wall, but you might be there all night. Because I'm not going to promise anything like that. For one thing, I doubt Dad's home yet. And for another, even if he is, I need to suss out what kind of a day they've both had at work first. If they're tired and stressed, forget it."

Maya slid off the wall and headed up the drive. "Anyway, thanks for the pep talk and I'll no doubt see you guys soon."

"You sure you won't come to the pictures with us?" asked Kerry.

"Honest, I'd better not. I told Mum this morning I was only going to the café after school. She'll go ballistic if I don't go home for tea when Brigid's made it for me."

"Good luck!" Kerry called as they walked off towards the cinema to meet some of the others.

"Thanks, I'll need it," Maya grinned cheerfully as she put her key in the lock and opened the door.

Once inside, she could hear the distant drone of the television and the clank of pans coming from the kitchen. Other than that, the house sounded pretty peaceful.

Nina Joshi poked her head around the kitchen door and acknowledged her daughter.

"Maya, just in time. Brigid's about to dish up. Have you had a good day at school?"

"Fine thanks, Mum. You're home early."

"Mmm. I just got in. I've brought some paperwork home for a meeting tomorrow which I'll tackle later. I wanted us all to be together for dinner this evening because your father and I want to talk to you."

Maya's heart sank.

Sighing, she walked through to the kitchen, where her father was sitting at the table alongside Ravi, who was engrossed in *The Simpsons* on the little telly on top of the dishwasher. Sunny sat opposite, looking sullen (*As usual*, Maya thought). Brigid and Nina bustled about the cooker, between them slicing bread and serving up a stew.

"Hi, Dad," said Maya a little warily. "I didn't expect to see you home at this time..."

"My last few appointments were cancelled," Sanjay explained, "so I managed to finish a little early for once."

"Will you not stay and eat with us?" Nina asked Brigid once the food was on the table and everyone was ready to sit down.

"No, thanks anyway, I have to get back myself," Brigid insisted, heading towards the hall for her bag and jacket. "I'll see you all tomorrow," she announced cheerily, giving a wave as she went.

As Maya sat at the table, Sanjay Joshi picked up the remote control for the TV and flicked the off button, causing both Ravi and Sunny to pull faces at each other and glare at their father.

"You know the rules," he said. "No TV while we're eating. And especially not tonight."

"What's so special about tonight?" asked Sunny.

"Well, your mother and I wanted to talk to you all about a holiday."

"Oh, wow, Daddy. Are we going to go on an

aeroplane again?" Ravi demanded, wide-eyed with excitement.

"Quite probably, Ravi."

"Brilliant!" Sunny cried. "When? Where? Will it mean I miss some school?"

"No, Sunny, you won't. We're talking about going away towards the end of the summer. We thought we'd maybe go to Spain for a couple of weeks. What do you think?"

Maya thought it was a rotten idea. The thought of spending so much time in the company of her little sister almost put her off her food. However, she didn't want to get on the wrong side of her parents by complaining, not tonight.

"That's great," she lied through gritted teeth. "When exactly?"

"We're not sure," her father carried on, obviously enthused by the idea. "It depends on what sort of availability there is. But we thought it would be nice to rent a villa somewhere, hire a car and tour round. I think we could all do with a break. Both your mother and I have had a busy time recently and it will do you good to have some time off before your big year of exams. And it'll be nice to do something as a family, don't you think?"

"Uh, yes," said Maya uncertainly.

"Excellent, well, we'll keep you posted."

Maya smiled. *This is the perfect opportunity to collar them about the festival,* she thought. *They're on good form tonight.*

"Actually," she said, "since you're both here, I wanted to have a word with you as well...."

"Can I stay at Lucy's this weekend?" Sunny suddenly butted in.

Maya looked daggers at her sister. She'd obviously had the same idea about making the most of their parents' benevolent mood.

"Sorry, Maya," Nina said, acknowledging that her daughter had been rudely interrupted. "What do you mean, Sunny?" she carried on. "The *whole* weekend?"

"Uh, well, Friday and Saturday. Her mother's invited me. They want to take us out for the day on Saturday to see some museums or something and it would mean getting up early and getting home late. So they thought it made more sense to stay."

"I don't see why not, Sunny," said Sanjay, looking at Nina who nodded her approval. "So long as Lucy's parents are taking you we don't have a problem with that at all."

"Thanks, Dad," Sunny smiled. She turned to Maya and gave her a superior smirk, then went back to eating her food.

"So anyway. Maya, what were you saying?" Nina asked.

Encouraged by their response to Sunny's request, Maya took a deep breath and began again.

"There's a music festival not too far from here the weekend after – it's at Dansby."

"Mmm, I think I've heard some of the youngsters talking about it at work," Nina nodded.

"Anyway, it's over two days and The Loud are playing and all my friends are going – you know, Kerry, Sonja..." Maya was careful to mention her more sensible friends, the ones she knew her parents approved of.

"There's a big camp site there so everyone's planning on staying overnight," continued Maya, gabbling now. "We've got two enormous tents, with loads of space and sleeping bags and stuff, and it'll be good fun and safe with the boys around and I'd really really like to go. What do you think?"

By the looks on her parents' faces, Maya knew immediately what they thought. No way. The relaxed, smiley faces in holiday-planning mode had been replaced by frowny, worried ones.

Nina spoke first, as she normally did in these situations.

"So tell me, Maya," she said in a voice Maya knew meant she was about to probe deeper, "this *festival*. What sort of music festival is it? And what sort of people will be going there, other than your friends?"

"People like me, Mum. Kids my age or older. Some younger," she added quickly. "You know, normal people."

Silence.

"And you're planning on spending the night in a tent. Will Alex be there?"

"Uh, yes. *No*. I don't know. To be honest, I haven't asked him."

"But assuming he is going, then he'll be staying with you? And your friends?"

"Yes, I guess so. But like I said, there are two tents. One for the boys, one for the girls."

Nina and Sanjay exchanged looks which perfectly matched each other and expressed the same emotion – complete disbelief.

"I think what your mother is trying to establish is that you are absolutely sure of the sleeping arrangements," Sanjay began. "And without wanting to sound patronising, we weren't born yesterday. We know as well as you do what young people get up to at times like this. I worry about the drunkenness, drugs, sex... Maya, I would hate to think that you might be tempted by friends who might not be as sensible as you..."

"Oh, come on, Dad..." Maya started to argue, frustrated that she wasn't being trusted to use her own judgement as usual.

"I'm only thinking of you, Maya," her father continued, holding his hand up to silence her objections. "I'm sure we can compromise. You say it's being held not too far from here. If that is the case, then why can't you just come home at the end of the first day, then go back the following morning, if you're so insistent on not missing anything?"

"But that's just not the same, is it?" Maya protested. "I'll have to leave too early to see the best acts and I'll miss out on all the fun..."

As soon as Maya had said that she knew she'd made a mistake. However innocently she meant the statement to be, she was virtually admitting that any 'fun' was to be had at night.

"I'm sorry, Maya," said her father, "I would like to agree, but I – we – simply can't. We would never forgive ourselves if anything happened to you because of someone else's rashness. I think you're much better off coming home on Saturday evening and returning on Sunday. I don't see the problem in that."

"But, *Dad*..." Maya began to protest.

Her father put up his hand again to silence her.

"No, Maya, there's nothing more to say. You do as I've suggested or you don't go at all. That's my decision and that's the end of it."

CHAPTER 7

● ●

DEKE ON THE PROWL

"I can't believe your old man lets you get away with mega house parties like this. Mine would throw a fit. How often did you say you stage these things?"

"Whenever I like," shrugged Matt. "To be honest, he's not around much – always away on business and stuff – so I've pretty much got the run of the place."

Deke looked around Matt's darkened den, unlit except for a powerful strobe and flashing coloured lights in front of his DJ decks. From what he could work out so far, there was Matt's own room, which was kitted out with his sound equipment, most up-to-date CDs and regular lads' hanging out stuff; there was a kitchen upstairs full of drinks and crisps; there was the conservatory, which was attached to the kitchen, and the garden, which was like an extension of the den in the open air. It was a great place for chilling out under the stars.

"Can't be bad. And your girlfriends are babes too," said Deke, his eyes following Maya as she wandered across the den towards Ollie and Kerry.

"Yeah, and she's taken," Matt pointed out.

"Shame. Anyone here who isn't? Maybe a Britney Spears lookalike?"

"Hmmm, well there's my mate, Sonja – she's a bit of a babe. But the only problem there is that she's got a long-distance boyfriend up in Newcastle."

"That's *his* problem, not mine," Deke laughed. "Where is she then?"

"Dunno, I haven't seen her yet. Hang on..."

Matt looked over to where Kerry, Ollie and Maya were chatting.

"Hey, Kez," he hollered. Kerry looked round and gave him a little wave. "Where's Son tonight?"

"She's not coming," Kerry called back. "She's got a really bad headache. She asked me to tell you. I was just waiting for the right moment. Sorry."

"No worries." He turned back to Deke. "She's a bit too much in *lurrve* anyway, mate, if you know what I mean. Actually, though, I've got a friend who's *sort of* a blonde bombshell. At least she is this week – she might have dyed her hair burgundy by the next time I see her."

Matt scanned the room looking for Cat. "Uh... there she is. In the skintight all-in-one and spiky boots."

"Yeah, I noticed her earlier," Deke nodded. "Seems a bit scary-looking to me."

"Cat? Nah, once you get past the mad clothes and hair, she's sound."

"I'll take your word for it, mate! Personally, I prefer a more natural look, where you don't get a mouthful of Max Factor when you snog 'em. What about her, the one who's just walked in. She's gorgeous."

Matt turned and followed Deke's line of vision to see that Anna was heading towards them. *Wow, you look amazing!* Matt thought as he watched her.

She was wearing a little floaty, layered silk dress with shoelace straps and matching strappy sandals. Her brown hair was piled on top of her head with wispy bits pulled out to frame her face. She wore only a little eye make-up and a dark, berry-coloured lipstick which emphasised her perfect mouth. Matt practically melted at the sight of her.

"Great!" Deke went on. "She's heading right

on over. I knew I looked good tonight, but I didn't expect to pull quite so easily."

"Uh, you haven't," Matt smirked, "That's Anna and she's *definitely* taken."

"Hiya. Missed me?" said Anna once she'd got close enough to plant a kiss on Matt's lips and stroke his face.

"Uh, right. I catch your drift," Deke chuckled, holding his hands up and backing away. "I'll have a scout around then. See you later!"

"Sure."

"What was all that about?" Anna asked innocently as Deke wandered off towards the kitchen.

"That's Deke," explained Matt, "the promoter. Remember he was in the café with me a couple of days ago?"

Anna nodded.

"He's after a bit of *lurrve* action tonight. I think he would have liked it to have been with you."

Anna moved a little closer and wrapped her arms around Matt.

"I hope you put him right on that score..." she said, her head raised towards him, her mouth drawn upwards into a little smile.

"Sure did," came the muffled reply as Matt buried his head into her neck and began kissing her.

Anna giggled. "Hey, that tickles!"

"S'meant to."

"Hey, you two lovebirds," Ollie interrupted, coming up and putting his arms around Matt and Anna, "any chance of putting some serious dance music on? Liven things up? This stuff is a bit girlie for me."

"Course, why don't you help yourself? I'm sure you can find something with a harder edge. In fact, I think I've still got your Charlotte Church CD here," Matt suggested sarcastically.

"*Ooh*, touched a nerve, touched a nerve," jibed Ollie mercilessly. "I see your mate Deke has turned up then," he added.

"Yeah," Matt nodded. "I think he might be someone worth keeping in touch with. He's got loads of contacts in the business and he was telling me he even booked some of the DJs for Dansby."

"Wow, really? I hope you put a good word in for yourself?"

"I tried, but he's already got it sorted. But you never know, do you? Something might come up in the future and if I keep tabs on him, I might get some work out of it."

Although Matt *sounded* a bit vague, what the others didn't know was that he was pinning his highest hopes yet on Deke.

● ● ●

"I asked Mum and Dad about going to Dansby the other evening," Maya told Alex as they headed towards Matt's kitchen.

"Uh-huh, so how was it?"

Alex helped himself to a beer from the fridge, flipped the top off using Mr Ryan's state-of-the-art bottle-opener, and came back to where Maya was standing in the doorway.

"Pretty dreadful really," she said, trying to smile but not feeling much like it. "I thought they'd be in a relaxed frame of mind, what with them talking about a holiday, but they gave me such a hard time. I know I wasn't expecting them to let me go, but all the same, I didn't think they'd get on their high horses quite so much."

"They weren't keen on letting you out on your own for the weekend then?"

"No and the thing that really got to me was that only seconds before, they'd agreed to let Sunny stay at her mate's house for the whole of this weekend. It's so unfair, letting her do what she wants, but not me. I can't believe it. And then they started grilling me about whether you were going. It was as if they were willing me to say yes so that their sordid minds could start working overtime."

"And what *did* you say?"

"That I didn't know. Which is true. I mean, we haven't really talked about it, have we?"

"No, I guess not."

"So?"

"So... you're asking me if I'm going?"

"Uh-huh."

"Well, I guess the honest answer to that is no."

"Oh."

Alex moved a little closer and wrapped his arms around Maya, kissing her lightly on the top of the head.

"Trouble is," he carried on, swaying them both gently to the beat of the music coming from the den downstairs, "at the risk of sounding like an old fart, I gave up all that being stuck in a muddy field with thousands of other mud-caked souls years ago. I don't think I can be bothered with it any more. Do you know where I'm coming from?"

"Um... circa 1970?" Maya suggested playfully, realising that he was sending himself up but still hugely disappointed.

Alex guffawed. "Hmmm, I suppose that's the kind of answer I deserve," he replied, scratching his chin. "It's true though. Sometimes I wonder what a happening young thing like you sees in an old crusty like me..."

"If you're fishing for compliments, you can forget it," laughed Maya.

"Oh." Alex pulled a face.

"I'm disappointed you're not going, but I can't say I'm surprised," continued Maya. "For someone of your age, lying on the floor in a damp old tent would play havoc with your back. No, you're better off staying at home with your pipe and slippers by a nice warm fire. Leave it to us *youngsters* to show the world what it's really like to live. You can watch it on the news and tut about the youth of today while you're tucking into your home-help tea and waiting for your bed-bath."

"Ouch! So does that mean you're still planning on going then?"

"Put it this way. I've got a week to use my powers of persuasion on Mum and Dad to get them to agree to let me go – on *my* terms."

"Well, if anyone can pull it off, you can."

Maya's face took on a determined look. "Don't you worry, Alex. I'm going to give it my very best shot."

CHAPTER 8

• •

UP CLOSE AND PERSONAL

"Phew, I'm *so* hot!" Kerry wafted the front of her long-sleeved T-shirt back and forth in an attempt to cool herself down. Matt's party was packed now and she was beginning to feel the worse for it.

"I know you are," answered Ollie, giving her an over-the-top, salacious look and wiggling his eyebrows up and down. "You don't have to tell me."

"Stop it, Ol, I'm blushing," Kerry squeaked, but didn't resist when he put his arms around her waist and eased her body towards his.

"Want me to make you even hotter?" he whispered, wrapping his arms around her and squeezing her tightly.

"Not unless you want me to faint," Kerry whispered back.

"At the sight of my God-like features, you mean?"

Kerry giggled. "'Fraid not. More from the fact that it's about 30 degrees in here. Sorry to burst your bubble and all that."

"Oh." Ollie's face took on a mock downcast look and he pretended to cry on to Kerry's shoulder. Normally, she would enjoy this kind of endearing behaviour from Ollie; tonight, however, the weight of his head plus the fact that he still had his arms around her was beginning to make her feel decidedly light-headed and woozy.

"Actually, Ol, before you get too cosy, I'm going to have to go to the loo," she said, not wanting to make a fuss, but keen to get away from the heat of his body for a few minutes.

Ollie stepped back and studied her.

"You are a bit pink in the face. Are you sure you're all right?"

"Honestly, don't worry," she soothed. "I just need the loo."

"Well, if you're sure."

"Yeah."

"I'll wait here for you."

Kerry headed off in the direction of the cloak-room in the hall. As much as anything she wanted a bit of space, away from the throbbing bodies all around her. The toilet sounded like a perfect haven. Plus she really was busting for the loo.

Unfortunately, the downstairs toilet was occupied and there was a queue of about four people waiting. Kerry walked straight past and headed for the one upstairs. Flicking the light switch on in the large bathroom, she walked in and closed the door behind her.

Heaven. The window was open so it was lovely and cool in there. Peaceful, too, compared to the throbbing noise and smoky atmosphere downstairs. Kerry went to the loo then filled the sink with cold water and splashed her face, drinking in a few cupped handfuls of water, grateful to be away from the hubbub for a few minutes.

She sat down on the plushly carpeted floor and began fanning herself with a towel. It felt fabulous – she was so relaxed she could have stayed there all night. Kerry closed her eyes and listened to the distant bass coming from beneath her.

Knock! Knock!

Kerry jerked her head up and sat bolt upright.

"Kez, is that you in there?" she heard Ollie hiss.

"It's unlocked," she hissed back, realising that she'd forgotten to put the catch on the door.

Ollie poked his head around the door and rushed inside, his eyes apprehensive at the sight of her.

"Are you OK? Did you faint?" he asked, seeing her sitting on the floor, her legs sprawled out in front of her.

Kerry began to laugh gently to herself. "No, silly," she said. "I sat here because it was nice and breezy under the window and I wanted to cool down. Come and sit next to me."

Ollie locked the door behind him and did as he was told.

"I got worried when you didn't come back," he explained. "Then I saw that queue and realised you might have come up here. You looked like you were about to pass out downstairs..."

Kerry turned and took his hand in hers.

"Aw, you're so sweet," she smiled. "It's much nicer up here though, isn't it? Away from the throng."

"Uh-huh." Ollie leaned over and kissed her lightly on the lips. "You know how much I love you, don't you, Kez?" he said suddenly.

Kerry smiled and squeezed his hand. "Yes, but you can tell me again if you like..."

"Well..." He thought for a moment. "I love you more than Posh Spice loves Beckham... uuh... more than Robbie Williams loves himself..."

"Oh, *wow*, Ol, *that* much?" Kerry mocked, snuggling into his chest. She felt so relaxed and happy that it seemed like the most natural thing in the world to begin kissing him, pulling him gently towards her as she did so. She could feel the softness of his lips on hers, the weight of his upper body pressed against her. He was wearing her favourite after shave, the smell of which seemed to come alive as the heat of her body increased, so close as it was to his now.

She moved one hand down his back and felt for the bottom of his shirt. She slipped her hand underneath and began to move it up his bare back, gently massaging his warm skin with the tips of her fingers. Kerry shivered as she felt his hand slide up her bent leg, stopping to skim the top of her knee, then sliding along the outside of her thigh to the top of her leg, where it stroked her warm skin gently, sensually.

Kerry closed her eyes as she felt Ollie's lips planting butterfly kisses of the lightest touch on her cheeks, eyes, nose, forehead. They were lying side by side now, their legs and arms entwined. Kerry could feel his heart beating fast against hers, could hear his breathing which was in tune with her own.

Closing her eyes once more, she sank happily into a moment she wanted to last forever.

• • •

"She's nice-looking."

Billy Sanderson, The Loud's guitarist, pointed his lager can in the direction of a slightly-built girl with dark hair. She was wearing a black leather jacket over a short, dark-red dress and was standing with a group of friends a few metres away from him. She looked vaguely familiar to Billy, but he couldn't place her.

"Hmmm, not my type, I'm afraid," Andy sniffed dismissively as he surveyed Matt's den for someone interesting to focus on. "Now *that's* more like it," he said, motioning to a tall, skinny guy with blond curly hair and a hard, chiselled face. "Sex on a stick, that one."

He chuckled merrily into his can and took a glug of beer.

"Have you never fancied girls?" asked Billy. "Not even the tiniest bit?"

Andy shook his head. "Nope."

"So I guess there's no chance of us falling for the same girl tonight then," Billy observed, smiling at his friend.

"Not unless you go for deep voices and a few days' stubble," answered Andy.

"I've been out with a few girls like that," Billy said, deadpan. "...Only once though."

Both boys cracked up at the thought.

"Actually," Billy carried on, "joking aside, I

could do with a bit of love interest – it's been ages since I snogged a girl. I'm beginning to forget how to do it."

"Do what, exactly?" Andy asked mischievously.

"Snog, you idiot," laughed Billy.

"Oh *that*. Well, speaking as an observer only, even I can see that there are some pretty fit girls here tonight. If I was that way inclined, I'd be well stuck in."

"Yeah, I know what you mean. But there's so many to choose from, I don't know where to start."

"How about that one over there?" Andy pointed to the girl in the red dress whom Billy had been admiring earlier. "I saw her giving you the eye a minute ago."

Billy turned to see that the girl was staring at him with intense dark eyes. Seeing that he was now watching her, she gave him a big smile and waved.

• • •

"Omigod, will you look at that?"

Anna's hands flew to her face, in a mixture of surprise and mock horror. She peeped through the gaps in her fingers, shook her head from side to side and then began to laugh uncontrollably.

"What? What is it?" demanded Matt,

grabbing her wrists and pulling her hands apart so he could see her face.

"Over there," Anna whispered. "In the hammock."

Matt peered out from the conservatory into the garden and saw the shadowy figures of two people illuminated by the night lights slung around the apple trees supporting his hammock. Sitting in the middle of it, swaying gently, and very much entwined, were Cat and Deke.

"After what you told me he'd said about her, I'd have thought they would be the two people least likely to get off with each other," Anna managed between giggles.

"Well, he didn't seem too interested at the time, but I guess that was before he met her."

"And if Cat had the hots for him, she'd soon let him know. And she'd give him no chance to get away, whether he liked her or not."

"Mind you," chuckled Matt as they watched Cat and Deke disappear into the folds of the hammock, "from where I'm standing it looks to me like he's not putting up much resistance."

• • •

Maya and Alex walked from the poplar trees at the end of Matt's garden back towards the brightly-lit house in front of them. Having wandered up there to enjoy a quiet moment to themselves, they ended up sharing a passionate kiss that had almost knocked Maya off her feet.

It was a lovely warm night and the smell of various scented flowers wafted in the air as they brushed past them. As they got nearer the house, nature gave way to human life; Maya could make out the shadowy figures of people inside the house and hear the dull buzz of voices talking, interjected with the odd shriek here and there as someone got enthusiastic about something or nothing.

They began to pick their way among bodies squatting, sitting or completely sprawled on the grass. As they walked towards the patio doors Maya spotted a group of people huddled together whom she vaguely recognised but couldn't quite place.

They looked incredibly glam, much more so than the people who usually went to Matt's parties. *Apart from Cat*, Maya thought, *who always looks like she's off to the Brits*. This little cluster of girls was equally tarted up in high heels, teeny tiny dresses, loads of jewellery and perfectly teased hairdos. They could easily be off for a night out at the most glamorous party in town, rather than an evening spent in Matt's back garden.

As she got closer, Maya squinted to try and make out who they were in the oddly-lit gloom. She was sure she recognised their faces... but where from?

Then it clicked. One of them was Lucy, Sunny's friend. *Hang on*, Maya thought, *Sunny's supposed to be spending the night at Lucy's house. So if* she's *here...*

Maya took a few strides closer, then stopped dead. The girl who had her back to Maya suddenly turned and leaned to talk into Lucy's ear.

Maya gasped as she realised with a jolt who it was.

Sunny.

CHAPTER 9

• •

LIES, LIES, LIES

Maya felt anger course through her body. She was livid. *Can't I go anywhere without Sunny butting in? Can't I even go to my mate's party without her getting in on the act? Is there no end to it?*

She watched Sunny and her oh so glamorous bunch of mates standing in the garden shivering in their skimpy clothes. They all looked a little nervous, despite the bravado, as if they didn't quite know what to do with themselves. *Who invited them?* Maya thought. *They don't know Matt... he's not a friend of any of theirs.*

With Alex a few paces behind her, she strode up to her sister and tapped her on the shoulder. "Sunny, I want to talk to you," she said, grabbing her sister's arm and pulling her away from her friends.

"Sure," Sunny replied, smiling a falsely sweet smile.

Even up close, Maya hardly recognised her sister. She looked so sophisticated with her well made-up face and her hair piled on top of her head. She'd obviously gone to a lot of trouble, colouring her hair so that it took on a reddish-brown sheen when she moved, and pulling out a couple of long, straight pieces which were dyed red and framed her face. She looked like a starlet ready to go on *Top of the Pops*. She also looked a good five years older than she really was.

"What the hell are you doing here?" Maya demanded.

Sunny gave her a look of disdain and replied, "What does it look like I'm doing – getting my legs waxed?"

"Who invited you?" snapped Maya.

"Matt did, actually," Sunny replied haughtily.

"You're kidding!" snarled Maya, her voice thick with disbelief. "Why on earth would he want to invite a bunch of girlies like *you*? I bet you've been nosing around my room or listening to my phone conversations. How else would you know about this party, you little snoop?"

She felt Alex's arm on hers and could sense that he had stepped in to get her to calm down. But it was difficult when Maya was so angry.

"Do Mum and Dad know you're here?" she demanded.

"'Course they do."

Maya felt the animosity well up inside her even more. Common sense told her that her sister was lying – there was no way her parents would allow Sunny to go to a party like this. But a small part of her was desperate to believe that was the case. It would added up, after all.

Maya knew Sunny was allowed much more freedom than *she* ever had, that was for sure. Just look at what had happened the other night when Maya was refused permission by her parents to camp over at the music festival, while Sunny was allowed to stay at her friend's for the weekend...

Aha! Maya suddenly realised, amazed that it hadn't dawned on her earlier. *Of course, that's how Sunny has been able to get here*.

"You liar, Sunny," Maya hissed. "Mum and Dad think you're at Lucy's for the weekend. That's the only reason you've managed to sneak here tonight. I expect you were lying to them about going to a museum as well, just like you lie about everything else."

"No, that was the truth," came Sunny's uppity retort. "We *did* go to a museum – God, it was so boring."

"So you say Matt invited you here?" Maya asked again.

"Yeah, more or less."

"OK, well you won't mind if I go and ask him about it then, will you?"

Sunny shrugged, turned away and sauntered back towards her friends.

"I could cheerfully throttle her," Maya spat to Alex as she steamrollered into the house in search of Matt. "She's driving me nuts. Every time I look behind me she's there, in my face, sticking her nose into my life, watching my every move. I feel like I'm being stalked. Now, where the heck is Matt?"

"Hey, come on, Maya, be reasonable. You don't actually believe he invited her, do you?" reasoned Alex.

"No. Yes. Oh, *I don't know*," Maya wailed. "I guess I know he wouldn't – I mean, he knows how I feel about her, everyone does. But... well, I just want to hear him *say* it, just to prove what a stinking liar she is. Ah..."

Maya broke off. She could make out the bright orange of Matt's shirt as he stood over by his enormous collection of CDs, sorting through them for something to play.

"Hey, Matt!" Maya called out as she got nearer.

He turned round. "Hi, Maya, having a good time?" he asked innocently.

"I was until I saw my darling little sister here," Maya replied, her face taut with tension.

"Huh?" Matt looked over one shoulder, then the other, before looking back at Maya. "Sorry?" he said. "*Who* did you say was here?"

"Sunny!" Maya nearly shouted. "She's here, in the garden, with her bunch of silly friends. She says you invited her. Is that true?"

Matt looked totally bemused. "Sunny? Your sister? Are you kidding? Who let *her* in?"

Maya relaxed. Matt didn't have a clue about Sunny's appearance at the party.

"Are you OK?" asked Matt. "You look like you're about to explode. You didn't really think I'd invite your sister, did you? Give me some credit."

"Oh, I'm sorry, Matt," Maya replied softly, bringing her hands up to her face to cover her embarrassment. She was grateful to feel Alex's arms slip round her waist and hold her tight, supporting her when she needed it most.

"Of course I didn't really think you had," she explained, "but that's what Sunny said had happened. I guess I just blew."

"That's OK, forget it," said Matt. "I don't know how she got invited or who let her in. If I'd opened the door I'd have sent her home. But look, if she's here, so what? Don't let it ruin your evening. That'd probably give her the biggest satisfaction, seeing you get all upset. Why don't you just leave it, ignore her even? Pretend she isn't here."

Maya gave a wry laugh. "I wish I could. But you're right, I shouldn't let her get to me. Hey, dig out *I Will Survive* by Gloria Gaynor and I'll get rid of my frustrations on the dance floor."

Matt pulled a face. "Gloria *who*? What are you trying to do – ruin my credibility?"

Maya laughed.

"Phew, thank God for that," Matt replied. "For a minute there I was scared. I was definitely seeing you in a new light."

"What, level-headed, analytical, never-lets-anything-get-to-her-Maya completely loses it? Is that the sort of thing you mean?" she mocked.

"Hmmm, something like that."

"I'll do my best not to disappoint you next time," she said. "But now, I'm going to take your advice, ignore the fact that Sunny's here and dance with Alex. Catch you later."

She turned round to face Alex, who still had his arms wrapped around her.

"Thanks for supporting me," she said, reaching up and kissing him lightly on the lips.

"Actually, I was acting more as a restraining

device," he joked, leading her off to find a space in among the dancing party-goers.

Maya giggled. "It's OK, I think I've calmed down now. Matt's right, I should just ignore her, pretend she isn't here."

"Yeah, so long as we keep a safe distance between you two, you need never know she's at the same party."

"Mmmm." Maya pulled him a little tighter and closed her eyes. They began to smooch, swaying gently back and forth in time to the slow track Matt had just put on. They stayed like this throughout the whole song, not speaking, just enjoying being close to each other. Maya relaxed and resolved not to have anything to do with her sister for the rest of the night.

CHAPTER 10

● ●

CAUGHT RED-HANDED

"So how's it going with Red Dress?"

Andy sidled up to Billy, who was grabbing a couple of cold cans from the fridge, and gave him a knowing look.

Billy smirked. "Fine," he replied.

"Only fine?" Andy queried. "She looks pretty keen to me."

"Been spying on us then?"

"Only to see if I can pick up a few pulling tips for future reference. From where I've been standing, you seem to have a pretty smooth chat-up technique."

"I do my best," Billy preened, laughing. "Actually, I think she's the one doing most of the chatting up. She's a right laugh."

"So do you fancy your chances?"

"I guess so. Like I say, she hasn't exactly given me the brush-off."

"And she hasn't taken her eyes off you since you came over here, either," Andy observed, looking over to where the girl they were talking about stood, her eyes glued to Billy's rear view.

"Really? I'd better get back then," grinned Billy. "I don't want to disappoint her by talking to a mutt like you all night, do I?"

Boffing Andy gently in the stomach, Billy took his lagers and sauntered confidently back to the petite girl eyeing him from a distance.

• • •

"Hell-lo... anyone in there?"

Kerry jumped away from where she'd been lying entwined with Ollie on the bathroom floor and sat bolt upright. She looked wildly from the rattling door handle to Ollie beside her. Laid-back as always, he merely grinned, propped himself up on his elbow and hollered, "Hang on a minute!"

Then he leaned over to a frantic-looking Kerry and kissed her on the knee.

"What are we going to do?" Kerry hissed as he got to his feet and pulled her up alongside him. "It's obviously someone wanting the loo. We can't leave together – it's too embarrassing."

"Well, unless you're up for shimmying down a drainpipe, I don't think we've got a lot of choice," laughed Ollie.

Kerry cringed as Ollie went and opened the door to the stranger on the other side. Trying to hide her face behind her hand, she studied the carpet, desperately wishing that it would part in the middle and swallow her up.

"Cheers, mate, I'm busting," the lad said, not giving them a passing glance as he rushed by.

Ollie led a still mortified Kerry out of the bathroom and on to the dark landing outside.

"Hey, look," the guy said, suddenly turning to them both as they headed away. "Uh... you guys haven't got any spare condoms on you, have you?" he asked a little sheepishly. "Only me and my girlfriend are about to leave and we've got nothing on us."

Kerry's felt her face turn beetroot and she came out in a hot sweat. "Uh... uh... um," she muttered.

"Sorry, mate," Ollie grinned. "Can't help you there."

"No worries. See you," the lad replied and shut the door behind him.

Ollie took one look at Kerry's face and threw his arms around her neck, burying his face in her hair and chuckling away merrily.

"Look at you," he said, drawing her towards him and hugging her close. "Like you're about to die of shame."

"I am," Kerry said and began to giggle too, her shoulders shaking gently against Ollie's chest. "I've always thought there was something a bit sordid about finding couples in toilets together. And now here I am – guilty of the very same thing."

"Aw, never mind," Ollie carried on, kissing the top of her head. He cupped her chin in his hand so that he could continue kissing her on the forehead, nose, lips. "It only makes me love you all the more," he continued between kisses.

Kerry smiled. "Thanks," she answered, wrapping her arms around him, her hands running up his back once more.

"So...uh, did you mean what you said back there... about not having any condoms?" she added, a little breathlessly now.

"Uh-huh."

"Shame," she whispered, blushing. *Because I'd really like us to take this further*, were the thoughts she didn't voice.

"Mmmm, I know what you mean," said Ollie, his hand stroking her hair away from one ear so that he could nibble the lobe with his trembling lips.

Kerry pulled away so that she could see all of his face, which she held between quivering fingers. She looked earnestly into his eyes. "I love you so much, Ol, I really do. We've been together for so long now and I keep thinking how it's getting harder to stop..." Her voice trailed off.

Ollie took her hand and kissed the tip of each finger, all the while looking longingly into her eyes. He knew what she was trying to say.

"I know," he answered. "But I think we need to plan it a little better, so that we're, uh... more prepared. Anyway," he added, pulling her close again so that he could feel her whole body against his, "there's plenty of time for us. Waiting a while longer won't hurt."

• • •

"Hey! Where have you two been? We haven't seen you for ages."

Spotting Kerry and Ollie walking past her in Matt's den, Maya tapped Kerry on the arm before she could wander off.

Kerry gave a little jump and whirled round. Her face was tinged pink and her hand had gone to her throat in surprise. "Sorry, Maya, I didn't see you there," she apologised. "I was miles away..."

"You looked it," Alex laughed. "You also look

guilty as hell, like you've been getting up to something you shouldn't have."

Kerry laughed nervously. *If only you knew*, she thought then blushed again.

"We went for a walk," Ollie fibbed. "Have we missed anything?"

Alex looked at Maya and stroked her bare arm affectionately. "Will you tell them or shall I?" he chuckled.

Maya raised her eyes skywards and pulled a face.

"What, Maya?" demanded Kerry. "What's been going on?"

"Matt's had some gatecrashers – well, one in particular, and her mates."

"Oh, yeah – who?" Kerry asked curiously.

"My darling little sister."

Kerry gasped with surprise. "You're kidding me, right?"

Maya shook her head.

"Sunny? Here? Where?" Kerry's head swivelled around the room to take a look. Seeing no sign of Sunny, she turned back and asked, "Is she still here?"

Maya shrugged. "I can't imagine she's gone home so soon, not after all the effort she's put into getting here. We had a bit of a confrontation when I saw her, but since then I've been avoiding her. I expect she's lurking in some corner with her friends. Not that you'd recognise her – she looks like she's had a make-over. I had to do a double-take myself."

"Oh, *no*, Maya, you must be furious," sympathised Kerry. "She doesn't leave you alone, does she?"

Maya smiled ruefully. "I *was* really mad at first. Then the boys persuaded me to chill out, so I have. And you know what? It's worked. I've kept out of her way and thankfully, so far, she's kept out of mine. So I've had a really good time. *Considering*."

"Good for you," Ollie added. "You're right not to let it get to you. She's got a real cheek turning up here like that, though, hasn't she? It's not as if she's friends with anyone else here."

"Certainly not me," sighed Maya. "But, like I said, I'm not letting her get to me any more. It's my middle of the year's resolution. I've just stuck to dancing the night away with Alex. Oh, wow, this is one of my favourite tracks. You guys coming?"

Maya took hold of Alex's hand and led him, Ollie and Kerry to the mass of dancing bodies in Matt's den. For once, she felt free of the stresses her home life had been causing her recently. Gyrating madly around a laughing Alex, she giggled and whooped and danced uninhibitedly for the next five minutes or so.

When the track had finished, Maya wiped the beads of sweat from her forehead and looked up at her boyfriend. She noticed a really weird expression on his face, a kind of horror mixed with tension. Maya turned round to see what had caught his attention.

Over in the corner of the room she could see Sunny. She had taken off her jacket since the last time Maya had seen her. Underneath it she was wearing the skimpiest, most revealing, dark-red dress – one that Maya had never seen before. And, to cap it all, she was kissing someone.

Ravenously.

Maya took a few steps closer to get a better view. Then she realised who the boy was.

Billy.

CHAPTER 11

●●●●●●●●●●●●●●●●●●●●●●●●●●●

BRIEF ENCOUNTER

Sonja paced up and down the windy platform at Winstead railway station and cursed the fact that Owen's train was now scheduled to be ten minutes late. Still, she figured it gave her time to rehearse her opening lines over and over in her head as she stared at the tarmac, kicking loose stones as she walked.

Owen, I've got something to tell you...

Every time she thought about what she needed to say, her stomach churned and she felt her mouth go dry with nerves. It wasn't like Sonja to be faint-hearted about life... but this was major stuff, the biggest crisis she'd ever had to face. No wonder she was anxious.

It'll be fine, he'll be cool, he'll understand, she kept repeating to herself as she relentlessly pounded the platform. Although Sonja didn't know what she was going to do about being pregnant yet, she was banking on Owen to support her, to put the whole mess into perspective and help her get through it. Once she'd spoken to Owen they could begin to sort things out. Or at least, that was the plan...

In her mind, Sonja ran the gamut of his possible reactions to the news for the thousandth time. *Shock*. That would be first. Sure, he'd be gobsmacked. (Who wouldn't?) This news would come completely out of the blue. But once he'd got over the initial shock she was sure that understanding, sympathy and finally the offer of support would be there. It wouldn't be in Owen's nature to behave in any other way.

Sonja's stomach lurched as she heard the train pulling into the station. Her head shot up and she scanned the carriages as they came towards her, then glided past, one by one, as if in slow motion. It was difficult to see where Owen was sitting, so she didn't know which direction to expect him from until he emerged almost in front of her.

Sonja's eyes fixed on to his as her boyfriend approached. He was wearing a smile so wide it filled his entire face. She saw it change to a look of puzzlement as he got nearer, then realised her own face must be mirroring the apprehension she felt inside. Sonja forced a smile and threw her arms around him.

"Mmmm," he murmured, "it's good to see you again. It feels like it's been forever."

"Me too."

They held each other like that, not speaking, just hugging, for ages. Sonja found herself welling up and had to force back the tears for fear of Owen noticing and saying something that would make her blurt out everything in an incoherent rush.

They began walking hand in hand towards the exit.

"Y'know, I couldn't believe my luck when they told us where the course was being held," said Owen breezily, gripping Sonja's hand tightly. "Such a result. Even if the hotel's crummy I'll bribe the others to say how great it is, so we can maybe come down here more often."

Sonja couldn't bear to hear him chatting away, oblivious to the bombshell she was about to drop. She had to stop him.

"Owen, I've got something to tell you..."

There, she had done it, gone past the point of no return. He would know something was up now. He had to.

Owen stopped walking and looked at Sonja searchingly.

"What's wrong?" he asked in a completely different tone of voice.

"Not here. Can we go somewhere so we can sit down?" Sonja tugged at his arm and they carried on walking.

"I *knew* something was up when I first told you I was coming down. I *knew* you weren't keen. What is it, Son?" he pressed.

"I'll tell you. But not walking along the road like this..."

"Let's go to the café then. Find a quiet table."

Sonja was adamant that they *did not* go to the End-of-the-Line. "No. Definitely not," she said. "I don't want any of the others butting in. I need you to myself for a while. Let's keep on walking. There'll be somewhere open in the Plaza."

They carried on in silence for a while and Sonja was aware that now it was her hand gripped tightly around Owen's.

"Have you met someone else?" he asked suddenly. "Is that what all this is about?"

"Oh, no, Owen. It's nothing like that. "There's no one else, believe me."

He brightened immediately and shot her an easy smile. "Well, it can't be anything too dreadful then, can it?"

Don't you believe it, Sonja thought miserably as they carried on their way.

They finally reached the café in the shopping centre in the middle of town. Owen ordered a café latte and Sonja a cappuccino, then they sat at a corner table and Sonja quietly thanked God that there was no one there she knew.

"So what is it you want to tell me?" asked Owen, keen to get this part of the conversation over with so they could catch up on their lives since they'd last seen each other over a month ago.

"Uh..." Now she was faced with it, Sonja desperately wanted to chicken out, to think of something innocuous to say that would appease Owen and let her off the hook at the same time. But there was nothing. Her mind had gone blank. In the end she just blurted out her news.

"I'm pregnant."

She scrutinised his face for signs of a reaction.

Owen's eyes flickered for a moment then he half smiled, the corners of his mouth twitching nervously.

"You're kidding, right?" he said, eyes firmly fixed on hers.

Sonja shook her head.

They sat in unbearable silence for a few seconds.

"Are you sure?"

Sonja nodded. "Yes," she said quietly.

Owen shook his head slowly, all colour drained from him his face.

"I don't know what to say... You're absolutely sure?" he asked again in a monotone, obviously completely shell-shocked by the announcement.

"Uh-huh."

"So... what, you've done a test?" Owen was trying to be practical, find out the facts, but the question irritated Sonja.

"Yes. And it was negative. But I know I'm pregnant. I can tell," she said in a clipped voice.

"How?"

"Well, my whole body feels different. And my period is *so* late and normally it's always on time, to the hour even. So I just *know*, OK?"

Owen sank back into his chair and gave a heavy sigh. "Oh, God, I can't believe you're telling me this..."

He sounded devastated and it made Sonja feel even worse.

"I can hardly believe it myself. It's not as though condoms are usually unreliable... maybe you didn't put it on right." Sonja knew she was trying to shift the blame out of defensiveness, but the suggestion only served to get Owen's back up.

"Come on, I'm not an idiot," he said indignantly. "Surely you trust me enough to be able to do that properly?"

"I suppose so," replied Sonja. "But it takes two to make a baby, you know. I'd have thought you'd have realised that."

Owen rubbed his eyes with his thumb and index finger. "Look, bickering isn't going to get us anywhere," he said wearily. "I'm just trying to take this in."

"You'll be asking me next if I'm sure it's yours!"

Owen tutted, rolled his eyes skywards and sighed.

"Sorry," Sonja said, immediately regretting her last comment. She felt incredibly stressed; the conversation wasn't going at all as she'd expected and she was taking swipes at Owen as a result. "That was unfair. Uh, look, I know this is a shock and I've had a few more days to take it in..."

Owen nodded.

"But the fact is, a baby changes everything," Sonja carried on. "What about my course, and me coming to live with you? I'm not sure about any of it any more. The most important thing I need to decide right now is what to *do* about this..."

She looked down at her stomach, anger all over her face.

Owen sat forward in his seat. "Well, *I* can't tell you what to do about it," he shrugged.

"What do you mean? Don't you *care*?"

I can't believe I'm hearing this, thought Sonja wildly. *He's washing his hands of the whole affair, treating it like it's my responsibility and mine alone.*

"No, it's not—"

Sonja cut off his response by pushing her seat back and standing up so that she was leaning over Owen. "Just forget it, all right?" she seethed. "You go back to your nice career and your life in Newcastle, and I'll deal with this by myself. Like I should have done in the first place. I just wish I'd never told you."

Grabbing her bag, she turned away from Owen and hurried out.

CHAPTER 12

● ●

TRUE CONFESSIONS

Cat staggered into the End late on Sunday morning and begged Anna for a strong black coffee. Looking around, she saw Kerry, sitting alone in the window seat, and tottered over.

"Ignore me today," she said cheerily. "I'm not worth talking to. I just need to sit here and vegetate for an hour or so."

"What do you mean?" giggled Kerry.

"I think I left my brain behind in bed. Or I might have left it at Matt's party, I'm not sure which."

"Late night?"

"Early morning, more like."

"So what happened? I saw you getting cosy with that guy. Deke, wasn't it?"

Cat rolled her eyes skywards. "God, I was so

humiliated! I spent most of the night calling him Geek. I can't believe it. And you know what? He didn't even say anything. It wasn't until Matt collared me late on in the evening to take the mick that I realised my mistake."

Kerry burst out laughing. "Cat, only you could do something like that and get away with it. Anyone else would get the knock back from a guy, but you have them coming back for more. How do you do it?"

Cat shrugged her shoulders and took a sip of the coffee Anna has just placed in front of her.

"So how long did you stay at the party after we left?"

"Uh... not sure. Oneish... twoish. Then we went back to his place. Ooh, Kez, you should have seen it – it was gorgeous. It's one of those warehouse apartments down by the river, really big and airy, and the decor was dead minimalist and trendy. The bedroom was the best though; there was just a massive, king-size bed in the middle of the room with floor to ceiling windows and wooden floorboards. Very macho and sexy."

Yeah and I bet I can guess what you got up to in there, Kerry thought, her cheeks pink.

"Weren't you worried about being on your own with him?" she asked, a little surprised at Cat's boldness. "I mean, it's not like you know him very well – or at least, you didn't before last night?"

"Oh, I wasn't on my own," Cat replied matter-of-factly. "Viks came with me, and a couple of others."

"But you and Deke were there... as a couple?" Kerry continued, keen to make sure she hadn't got hold of the wrong end of the stick.

"Uh-huh."

"So do you really like him then?" asked Kerry innocently.

"He was a good laugh, but I'm not sure if he's my type really."

"Will you see him again?"

"Dunno. I've got his number, I know where he lives. We'll see."

"You're amazing," Kerry went on. "You're so cool about guys and relationships, so kind of laid-back and seemingly not bothered either way."

"That's because I've never met anyone I've been seriously into. Not really. I do believe in love at first sight but it obviously hasn't happened to me yet, although I've had my fair share of *lust* at first sight." Cat wiggled her eyebrows and grinned. "But when I do get hit by the big thunderbolt, believe me, I bet I'll be just as anxious for it to work as anyone else."

"I guess so," sighed Kerry. "You know, it

makes me realise how lucky I am to have Ollie. Sometimes I have to pinch myself to believe it's for real. I never expected to fall so deeply in love with anyone so soon in my life."

"Didn't you?"

"No way! I mean, come on, before Ollie there was no one. Then all of a sudden I find I'm with this guy who I love with all my heart, and who I know feels the same way about me, and it's just... so..."

"Sickeningly perfect?" suggested Cat, flashing another cheeky grin. "No, I'm joking. I think it's great what you've got; you're obviously made for each other."

"We are," Kerry agreed. "And the thing that makes it even more amazing is that well y'know, although nothing's happened yet between us, I can feel that it's getting closer and closer and it's so exciting, like we're about to go into unknown territory. Or, at least, that's how it is for me because I know Ollie's..." she broke off, searching for the right word to describe him.

"More experienced..." Cat finished for her.

"Yeah, that's it. But even so, these days, every time I'm with him we're finding it harder and harder to stop ourselves and it's like..." Kerry stopped again, her face suddenly crimson with embarrassment. "Oh, God, Cat!" she blustered.

"I didn't mean to say all that. You won't tell anyone will you...?"

"Of course I won't. I think it's really sweet. It proves that true love does exist. And it's great that you've both waited until the time is right. So are you saving it for when you go to Ibiza together?"

"Uh, not deliberately," Kerry answered. "But I can see it happening then."

"Right. Well, I'll tell you what you *should* do if you want it to happen then..."

"Go on..."

"Make sure you take some condoms with you and stick one under his pillow, or in his wash bag. Anywhere he'll find them – you know? *Then* he'll cotton on to where you're coming from. Take it from me, hon," she added mischievously, "it works every time."

Kerry burst out laughing. "I'll take your word for it, Cat. Actually, the only thing I'm kind of curious about now is what sex is really like... because I've got no idea."

"You watch the telly, don't you?" giggled Cat. "People are always at it on the telly. My mum cringes if we're in the same room together; she's so uptight about it all."

Kerry frowned. "I know, but everyone knows that's not for real – it's all camera angles and fake and soft focus and... well, not real life. *Is* it?"

"I don't know what you're asking me for," Cat said dismissively, "*I* don't know."

"Oh, I've read articles about it, Cat," Kerry rattled on. "It takes hours for the director to shoot a sex scene, and sometimes actors wear body stockings so you can't see their bits, and they get told what to do, down to the tiniest movement. It's totally unreal..."

"No, hang on, Kerry, you've missed my point," giggled Cat. "What I'm trying to say is that I don't know what *sex* is like..."

Kerry peered into Cat's innocent eyes and her mouth fell open. "*Don't* you?" she said in a barely audible voice. "You mean you haven't...?"

"No, I *haven't!*" Cat cried. "Omigod, did you think I *had*?" she demanded.

Kerry fidgeted nervously in her seat. "Er, well, yes, I guess I did."

"You're kidding me!"

"Look, I'm really sorry, Cat," Kerry was flustered. "I didn't mean to offend you. I just assumed..."

Cat sat in silence for a moment, her brain working overtime, trying to take in what she'd just heard.

"Um... I suppose I can see that people might think I'm not a virgin. I mean, I do tend to give the impression sometimes that I'm a bit of a man-eater. But, to be honest, it's all just a show."

"I guess that's where the confusion comes from..." said Kerry gently.

"And I am a flirt," Cat went on, "but most of the time it's just a big act. I mean, take what happened with Zac. He dumped me because he thought I was rubbing his face in it by flirting with guys in front of him."

"I remember," Kerry said.

"When the reality was, I meant nothing by it. I was just showing off."

"And you do get carried away sometimes," added Kerry helpfully.

"Yeah, but it's only a bit of a laugh," Cat explained. "That's not how I really am."

"No, of course not."

"Anyway, people can think what they like about me," said Cat, suddenly defiant. "It doesn't really matter. The only big deal is what *I* think about myself. It might not come across like this all the time, but I do have a lot of respect for myself and wouldn't jump into bed with *any* guy unless I was really sure."

"And you obviously haven't met the right one yet."

"Oh, God, no, might not until I'm forty. Who knows?" said Cat cheerily.

"But you do come across as being so...

97

experienced," Kerry tried to justify why she'd made such an assumption about her friend. "And the way you talk so matter-of-factly... like all that stuff about condoms... You can see why people get the wrong impression."

"But that's just it – I was *joking*!" Cat replied, a little frustrated. "It's all a load of bluster. It goes with the image."

"You mean it's all part of the act."

"Exactly. Pass the Oscar!"

"And you really haven't ever done it in your life? Never ever?"

"Nope."

"You know, it's going to take me a while to get used to this huge revelation about you, Catrina Osgood," admitted Kerry. "I think I'm going to be seeing you in a completely different light from now on."

"You mean one with an ethereal white glow and a halo around it?"

"Uh-huh."

"Doesn't really go with the make-up, does it?"

Kerry shook her head and they both collapsed into fits of giggles.

CHAPTER 13

• •

CONFRONTATION

"Hi, Maya."

Aware that he was standing directly in front of her, and cursing the fact that he would have to be the one person she'd bump into, Maya looked straight through Billy Sanderson to Anna who was standing behind the café's coffee machine during a short lull in Sunday afternoon trade. Maya sidestepped him and walked up to the counter.

"Hi, Anna," she said in an overly cheerful voice. "Have any of the others been in?"

"Yeah, Cat and Kerry were here earlier but they left about an hour ago. Matt's been in a few times. No one else. Except Billy," Anna added, nodding towards him, sitting in the window seat, with a mystified look on his face. It was evident that Maya's behaviour was puzzling him.

"Right. Sorry Alex and I left so abruptly last night," added Maya. "But I had to go or I might have said or done something I regretted. That's why I'd hoped to catch up with everyone. To apologise."

"That's OK," Anna smiled and thought back to the scene where Maya had seen her sister snogging Billy. Anna hadn't witnessed Maya's reaction, but Ollie said later that he'd never seen her look so angry. Apparently, she'd stormed off the dance floor, grabbed her things and left without saying goodbye to anyone. A frazzled-looking Alex had chased after her and neither of them had been seen again.

"Anyway, I'd better get on," continued Maya. "I've got the pleasure of escorting Ravi to a birthday party this afternoon. I'll catch up with you in the week."

"Sounds like hell on earth to me," Anna laughed. "But have a good time. Don't get covered in jelly, will you?"

Smiling, Maya turned back and, eyes focused strictly on the door and nothing else, strode purposefully towards it.

"Maya!" Billy called.

She blanked him completely, opening the door and escaping outside into the warm sunshine.

"Maya!" Billy leapt up from his seat and chased out of the End after her. He caught up with her charging down the road like a raging bull and began to walk beside her.

"What is it?" he pleaded. "Why are you ignoring me? Have I done something to upset you?"

Maya rounded on him, her nostrils flared.

"Are you kidding me that you don't know?" she fumed, stopping in the middle of the pavement and thrusting her hands on to her hips.

"Sorry, I haven't got a clue," shrugged Billy.

"Last night, at the party. What the heck do you think you were doing?"

"Having a few beers, dancing, chatting... the usual kind of things you do at a party," he replied, frown lines etched into his face. "What's the big deal?"

"The big deal to me, though obviously not to you, is that you were getting off with my sister, Sunny."

Billy's mouth dropped open and virtually hit the floor. "Oh, God!" he wailed, slapping his hand to his forehead in horror. "Of course!"

"What d'you think you were playing at?" Maya continued, her voice tight with anger.

Billy clasped his hands behind his head in shame. "I can't *believe* I was so stupid," he said, as much to himself as to Maya. "I *knew* I recognised her from somewhere... but, well, I was a bit drunk..."

"But not too drunk to take advantage of my little sister."

"Come on, Maya. *Hardly,*" protested Billy. *"She* was the one doing most of the chasing – you ask Andy, he was there too. Look, I'm really sorry, I would never have gone after your sister if I'd known who she was. But she looked so *different*. And anyway, she told me she was seventeen and she said she was called Sunita. I thought your sister's name was Sunny..."

Billy's voice trailed off and he shook his head from side to side in disbelief.

"I know it sounds ridiculous now," he carried on, "but I just didn't make the connection. She told me she went to college in the city. How was I to know she was lying?"

Now Maya knew Billy was telling the truth. She could just imagine Sunny spinning a yarn like that, the lies rolling out of her mouth – it came so much more easily to her than being honest.

"Did she really say that?" Maya quizzed.

"'Fraid so."

"God... you know, I'm so fed up with her," sighed Maya, "I've half a mind to tell Mum and Dad. They'd be horrified if they knew what she's been getting up to. To be honest, Billy, I think I'm more mad at the fact that she was at the party at all, than because of what happened between you two. She's got such a cheek and last night wasn't even half the story..."

"Has she been giving you lots of grief then?" Billy asked, leaning against a shop window, keen to talk.

"Sure has."

Maya found herself telling Billy about the run-ins she'd had with Sunny in recent months – of the lies she told, her constant sneaking on Maya, the smoking and, to top it all, seeing her bold as brass at Matt's party.

"No wonder you were angry," he said when she'd finished. "Last night sounds like the final straw."

"Yeah, but d'you know what the worst thing about all this is?" Maya asked. "It's that I'm dead jealous of her."

"Huh? What on earth for?"

"Because she's always allowed to get away with so much more than me. My parents don't seem at all bothered that she doesn't try at school and she always seems to get what she wants from them. I, on the other hand, have gone through my entire life having it drummed into me to be a high achiever. My parents have been so strict, pressurising me to get good grades, not letting me go out, frowning on the idea that I should *ever* have some fun. I tell you Billy, it's driving me nuts and I'm getting sick of it."

"Mmm," Billy mused. "It does seem hugely unfair."

"It is. But you know what?" said Maya, her eyes lighting up and a grin spreading over her face. "I've just thought of a way to redress the balance a bit."

"Go on," Billy said, a little nervous of what she was going to come out with.

"If *she* can get away with it, so can I. I'm damn well going to the Dansby festival and I *will* sleep with you lot in tents. And to hell with what my parents think about it."

CHAPTER 14

●●●●●●●●●●●●●●●●●●●●●●●●●●●●●●

ROWS AND REMORSE

"Hi! I didn't expect you to be here so early. I thought you were meeting Sonja?" Opening the door to her flat to let Owen in, Anna immediately noticed that he didn't look his usual upbeat self.

"Hi, sis," he said, "good to see you." He walked into the flat, gave her a kiss on the cheek, slung his rucksack on to the floor and slumped in the nearest chair.

Owen was tempted to blurt out the news to his sister right there and then. He could do with having someone on whom to offload the worry. But it wouldn't be right. At the moment, instinct told him to keep this bombshell to himself. It was up to Sonja if she wanted to tell people, but *he* wasn't going to.

"Uh, I did meet Sonja," he explained, "but she

wasn't feeling too well. And to be honest, I'm pretty knackered myself. So we cut it short."

"That's a shame. Mind you, she hasn't looked right for a few days. And she didn't make it to Matt's party last night," replied Anna, studying Owen intently. He did look drained. His face had taken on a kind of grey pallor and he looked about ten years older than when she had seen him last.

"You look all done in," she soothed. "They must be working you too hard. Let me make us both a coffee – the kettle's just boiled."

Anna went into the kitchen area to do so, bringing back two steaming mugs into the living room. Owen was staring into space, so much so that he didn't even see her standing in front of him, waving the mug in front of his face.

"Owen? *Owen?* Are you sure you're all right?" she asked, concerned now that it wasn't just overwork that was causing him to look so dreadful. He seemed so preoccupied.

"Huh?" Owen finally realised she was speaking and held up his hand to take the mug. "Sorry, Anna, it's been a tough week."

Anna was worried. When she had spoken to him yesterday to finalise the arrangements for today, he had been really upbeat about the course. What could have changed his mind so dramatically between then and now?

"Was Sonja feeling really poorly then?"

Owen started at the mention of his girlfriend. He hadn't heard the rest of the sentence, only "Sonja" which had made him jump and slop his drink.

"Ooh, sorry, Anna," he said, leaping up and rushing to get a cloth. "I was miles away."

What's gone on between you two, wondered Anna, aware from his reaction that the problem was nothing to do with work. He came back from the kitchen with a cloth and mopped up the splodges of coffee on the carpet. Throwing the cloth on to the table, he slumped back in his chair once more.

"I was just asking how Sonja was."

"Fine, great..." Owen's voice trailed off and they sat in silence for a moment, him not willing to say any more, her not daring to probe any deeper.

"Look, Anna, d'you mind if I have a bath?" he asked, standing up and placing his mug on the coffee table. "I feel really grimy from the train. Is that OK?"

"Sure you can. I'll, uh, make us something to eat, shall I?"

Owen didn't answer. He'd already picked up his rucksack and headed off to the bathroom, closing the door firmly behind him.

• • •

Maya walked into her house after her conversation with Billy and right into Sunny, who was eating crisps and watching TV at the kitchen table. Her hair was back to its natural colour, there was no trace of make-up on her face... she looked like Maya's younger sister once more. Glancing up, Sunny's mouth immediately turned down into an expression of contempt and she quickly looked away again.

"Where're Mum and Dad?" Maya barked, determined to have a go at her sister, yet careful to make sure they weren't in earshot.

"Mum's at Sainsbury's, Dad's in the shed," came the reply.

"Good. Did you have a nice time at Matt's last night?" Maya continued, her tone sarcastic.

Sunny shrugged. "It was OK."

"And you had a *nice* time snogging Billy?"

"Was that his name?" Sunny asked, her face registering no reaction. "I don't remember."

Maya dragged out a chair opposite Sunny and sat down. "So you won't remember lying about your age or telling him that you were at college in the city plus whatever other rubbish came out of your mouth?"

Sunny looked blankly at her sister. "Sorry,

you've lost me," she said haughtily. "You must be talking about someone else."

"Actually no, Sunita, I'm talking about you," replied Maya coldly. "And I'm getting pretty sick of either hearing or seeing what a lying, sneaky little cheat you're turning into. I've been pretty good to you so far. I haven't said a word to Mum or Dad about any of the rotten tricks you've pulled. But – and this is a warning – I've had enough."

"Who cares?"

"I do. You really showed yourself up last night. You looked like a tart and you behaved like one too. And quite what you were doing there in the first place, I can only guess at. I don't know if you're trying to prove how grown up you are or if you're just doing it to annoy me – either way, you're pushing your luck." Maya pushed her angry face close to her sister's. "If you pull any more stunts like that, or if I hear you've been telling any more lies, then Mum and Dad will hear about it. And that isn't a threat, it's a promise. Got that?"

Sunny merely shrugged again and carried on eating her crisps.

● ● ●

Phew.

Sighing deeply, Owen sank into the steaming hot water, slid down the bath and dunked his head underneath. He lay there for a few seconds, holding his breath and enjoying the welcoming feeling of the water lapping around him. When he came up for air he could feel his body throbbing with the heat of the water. It matched his head, which had been pounding since the encounter with Sonja earlier that afternoon.

He wasn't sure if her news had sunk in yet. He was still in a 'pinch me and I'll wake up' dreamlike state, except in his case it was a nightmare.

Pregnant, he thought. It really was a nightmare. He didn't want to be a father, not yet. What about his career? His *life*? It would change beyond all recognition with a baby around. And even more so for Sonja he suddenly realised.

God, what must she be going through? he thought and sorely regretted the way he'd handled things earlier. The bitter words of their conversation were whirling round and round in his head. He hadn't been the most understanding boyfriend in the world, of that there was no doubt. But the shock of the announcement had taken him by surprise. And he felt that the ensuing conversation had run away from him, out of control.

He hadn't meant to give the impression he

didn't care – of course he did. And he hadn't meant to get Sonja's back up, but she was so on edge, ready to jump down his throat at the first opportunity. *Not that I can blame her,* thought Owen.

If he'd been given a chance to mull it over – as he was doing now – he wouldn't have said half the things he did that afternoon. Wouldn't have said *any* of them.

Poor Son, she must be in a right state. And I haven't done a single thing to make her feel any better.

CHAPTER 15

● ●

HIGHS AND LOWS

The four members of The Loud were spread across the stage in the function room at the back of The Swan, Ollie's parents' pub. They were in the middle of one of the extra rehearsals they'd organised for the music festival on Saturday, which was going to be the biggest event of their lives so far.

There was a definite edge to their performance. They'd all noticed it. Since they'd been booked for the festival, they'd more than doubled their normal rehearsal rate and were practising Joe's new song, plus trying out new arrangements for some of their old songs. So far it was working and they were gaining confidence and technique each time they came together as a group.

Ollie's only worry now was that they still

hadn't heard anything from Saul, the promoter who'd booked them. It had been a week now since that first – and only – phone call, and Ollie was beginning to fret that he really had been set up. He tried hard to push the thought to the back of his mind.

"So, have you spoken to Meg since she got back from her hols?" he asked Joe during a break.

Joe practically glowed at the mention of her name. "Yeah," he answered, "I called her this morning. We're meeting up later..." His voice trailed off. It still felt weird to him talking about a girlfriend; it certainly didn't come naturally as it did to Ollie or Matt.

"And did she miss you?" Ollie probed, an impish grin on his face.

"Uh, yeah, she said she did," replied Joe, blushing. "Oh and she's definitely coming to Dansby at the weekend; she's dead excited about it."

"Does she know about... y'know... the song?"

"Uh, not yet, but she will..."

"You mean you're actually going to tell her?" Ollie said, wide-eyed. "Joe, that's great! It's about time you got the credit for all the stuff you write."

"I guess so," Joe flushed. "I only hope she likes it..."

"Ollie! Phone call for you." Joe's voice was

drowned by the booming tones of Ollie's father coming from the next room.

"Cheers. I'm on my way! She will, mate," he called back to Joe as he disappeared. "She'll love it."

He jogged through the bar to the telephone. It was at times like this, when he was rushing from one end of the building to the other, that he wished The Swan had one of those cordless phones you could wander around with. But, as his Mum so practically pointed out, it wouldn't last two minutes in a pub before someone pinched it.

When he came racing back in minutes later, Ollie's face was flushed with excitement. "Hey! You will *not* believe who that was," he yelped to the others.

Andy stroked his chin as though thinking hard. "Robbie Williams? Ali G?"

"No, you wally, only that bloke Saul, the festival promoter."

The others immediately sat up and took notice.

"He was calling to finalise the details for Saturday," shrieked Ollie. "And he wanted to know where to send the backstage passes. Can you bloody well believe it?"

"Oh, wow, that's brilliant! " Joe enthused.

"Yep," Ollie went on. "The festival kicks off at midday on Saturday and we're on the second stage at 1.30 pm for a twenty-minute set. Apparently we need to be there early in the morning to soundcheck and because we're on so early I reckon there'll probably only be about ten people in the audience, but who cares? It's a step in the right direction, eh, lads?"

The others nodded enthusiastically.

"Right," Ollie carried on, "I must phone Kerry to tell her the good news. I was beginning to wonder if it was someone's sick joke. I've got to tell her it's kosher after all."

He ran back into the pub again, leaving the other three to get excited about the prospect of playing on the same bill as bands who brought out proper albums and got into the charts.

Ollie dialled the Bellamys' number and sat at the bar waiting for an answer. Kerry picked up the phone.

"Kez, it's me," he chirped.

"Oh, hi, Ol," she replied. "Just hang on a minute will you, there's someone at the door."

Ollie heard Kerry put the receiver down and pad off towards the front door, then he heard the distant sound of female voices. Moments later, he heard Kerry pick up the phone again. He got ready to launch into his brilliant news.

"Ol, I'm going to have to call you back," she told him abruptly.

"Hey, Kez, it'll only take a second," he laughed. "I just wanted to tell you..."

"No, Ol, *really*," she cut in, uncharacteristically firm. "I have to go, it's important. I'll call you back later, OK?"

With that the phone line went dead and Ollie was left wondering what could be more important than his big news.

● ● ●

When Kerry answered her front door to find Sonja sobbing on the step, she knew something major was up. Like *big* time.

She had hardly ever seen Sonja cry in all the years that she'd known her. And yet here she was on Kerry's doorstep, tears coursing down her face, sobbing uncontrollably. Kerry threw her arms around her and dragged her indoors.

"Son, tell me, what is it?" She knew it must be something truly awful, but couldn't bear to think what.

After hanging up on Ollie, Kerry steered Sonja up the stairs to her bedroom, sat her on the bed, then grabbed a box of hankies from her dressing table and knelt down on the carpet in front of her.

Sonja took the tissue Kerry was offering and blew her nose. She grabbed another couple, pressed them to her eyes and took a deep breath.

"S-s-sorry about that," she sniffed, wiping her nose. "I was f-fine until I g-got here, then I just f-fell apart."

"What on earth is the matter? I've never seen you in such a state."

"Oh, Kez, this is so awful I don't know if I can tell you..."

"Tell me what?"

"I've just been out with Owen and I told him and he was s-s-so *horrible*. I couldn't believe it. I never thought he'd react the way he did, b-b-but he didn't *care*. And now I don't know what to do. I couldn't go home, everyone's there and I can't face them, not like this. So I came here instead. You don't *mind*, do you?"

"No, of course not," Kerry soothed, looking at her friend and wondering what she was going on about. "You'll be fine here, stay as long as you like. But what was it that you had to tell Owen that made him so mad?" she probed.

"Well... the thing is, *oh*, Kerry, the thing is... I'm pregnant. And I don't know what to do."

"What??!!" *No! Did I hear right? Pregnant? Not Sonja, of all people!* "God, Son... You must be terrified," Kerry got up off the floor and threw her arms around her best friend again.

"I am. It's the worst possible thing that could happen. I've completely ruined my life and I feel so miserable I could *die*."

Sonja began sobbing again, only this time into Kerry's corkscrew-curly hair. Kerry sat and hugged and rocked her friend, letting her know she was there for her in any way she could.

"What a mess," Kerry soothed, "And you're sure it's not just that your period's late?"

Sonja shook her head. "No."

"Have you been to the doctor's?" Kerry asked gently.

"How can I?" Sonja wailed, "I can't face Dr Joshi. How can I sit there and discuss that kind of thing with Maya's father? I *couldn't*, I'd be so embarrassed."

"Oh, God, of course," muttered Kerry.

"And what makes it even more unbearable," Sonja went on, "is that when I told Owen I thought we'd be able to sort it out. But he was just h-h-horrid."

"What happened? What did he say?"

Sonja related the conversation she'd had with Owen earlier. Kerry sat and listened and shook her head, totally sympathetic to Sonja's reaction.

"You know," Sonja finished, "I thought it might help if Owen was there for me. But he wasn't. He was a complete bastard and that upsets me more than anything."

Kerry nodded in agreement. "So do you know how pregnant you are?"

"I think so. It must have happened when I went up to Newcastle to stay with him, though God knows how it *did* happen. It's not as though we're both idiots. We both know all about safe sex. It must have just been a freak accident."

"And do you know what you're going to do about it?" probed Kerry gently.

Sonja's bottom lip began to wobble again. "N-n-no, not really. I mean, I know I don't want a baby, not *now*. I'm not even eighteen. But I don't know if I could get rid of it either. I mean, I suppose I could have it adopted but.... oh, God, I can't believe I'm having this conversation. My mind's all messed up, I honestly don't know what to do."

Kerry stroked her friend's hair and hugged her once more. "I'm sure. It's a lot to think about. But couldn't you try going to the Family Planning Clinic? They're there to help you and Dr Joshi need never know. I'll come with you, if you like. It might even be worth talking to Owen again, when he's had time to let the news sink in. I bet he's feeling really bad about what went on between you today..."

She broke off, aware that Sonja was shaking her head furiously.

"No way, Kerry," she said through gritted teeth. "I'm going to get through this on my own. As far as I'm concerned, Owen and I are finished."

CHAPTER 16

● ●

WAITING

I can't go on this course without trying to make amends. And I can't leave her thinking she's got to go through with this on her own.

Owen jumped out of the chair he'd been sitting in for the past hour and headed towards the door.

"I'm just nipping out for some beers," he said to Anna as he put on his jacket.

"Sorry, Owen. I should have got some in," she said, watching him intently and thinking how he didn't look as if the bath had improved things much.

"Don't worry," he said, opening the door and looking back at her staring face. "D'you want anything while I'm out?"

"Uh, no thanks."

Owen closed the door behind him and jogged down the metal staircase. *She knows something's up*, he thought. He could see it in her face and by the way she was watching his every move back there. Owen desperately wanted to unburden himself to Anna, but knew it wasn't fair. Not yet, not until he'd got things sorted with Sonja.

He'd decided he would ring her. Originally, while he'd been soaking, he had contemplated going round to her house, but decided against that move in case her family were around and wondered what was up. So he would have to phone her and beg her to see him again, to try and make amends.

Owen knew time was tight. He had to catch an early train in the morning to get to the hotel in the city for a 9 o'clock start, then he figured he wouldn't get the chance to make contact again until the course finished on Wednesday, not with the amount of lectures, meetings and working dinners he was expected to attend. So it was now or... too late.

Owen walked along the road to the off-licence and bought four cans of lager, buying time while he decided what he was going to say. Then he nipped over the road to the park and found himself a spot inside the gates where he wouldn't be overheard by anyone.

He drew his mobile phone out of his jacket pocket. As he punched in Sonja's number, he noticed his hands were shaking. Someone picked up at the other end almost immediately.

"Hello, is that Mrs Harvey?"

"No, it's Karin. I'll get her for you."

"Uh, no, actually it's Sonja I'm after. It's Owen."

"Oh, hi, Owen, how are you?" said Sonja's older sister cheerfully.

She hasn't told her family then. "I'm fine," he replied. "And you?"

"Couldn't be better. Uh, Sonja's not here."

Damn. "Oh, right. You don't know where she is, do you? Only I wanted to speak with her before I leave town tomorrow."

"No, I don't. I haven't seen her all day. Can I give her a message?"

"Um, could you say I rang and I've got my mobile switched on if she could call me."

"Sure."

"Thanks, Karin."

"Bye, see you soon."

I hope so, Owen thought as he pressed *End* and headed back to the flat.

• • •

Joe walked along the high street towards Burger King, where he had arranged to meet Meg after band rehearsal. She had wanted to come to The Swan, to hear him and The Loud play, but Joe had said no. He knew they'd be rehearsing *Moving On* and he didn't want her to hear it until Dansby.

He knew that once Meg told everyone the song was for her, they'd want to know if he'd written more of the band's material. Joe would say yes. And be proud. The days when he'd have died of embarrassment rather than let on he wrote songs seemed so very far away. Now, he decided, he'd be pleased that other people – his friends – knew.

As Joe walked towards Burger King, his eyes focused on the dark-haired girl standing at the corner of the street. He knew it was Meg – he could tell even from a distance. As he got closer she turned to look up the road and saw him, then hurried towards him, a broad smile on her face.

You're so gorgeous, thought Joe, his feet suddenly off the ground, his body feeling as if it was floating a metre or so above the pavement. *I can't believe you're mine*.

They were standing facing each other now, both smiling, neither speaking. Then, in unison, they leaned forward and kissed each other on the lips. It was electric. Joe could feel the tiny sensitive hairs all over his body tingling.

"So, did you have a good holiday?" he said when they finally broke away.

"Mmm, it was OK," Meg replied. Then giggled. "Actually, I spent most of my time thinking about you."

"Sounds scintillating," said Joe, a self-deprecating grin spread all over his face.

"Believe me, it was." Meg smiled naughtily, then took his arm in hers and steered him along the street once more. "So tell me, what's been going on with you while I've been away."

Joe went into enthusiastic detail about the upcoming music festival, about how all the band were dead excited and preparing madly for their big moment.

"And it's so great that you're coming," he finished, "because I've got something I want you to hear on the day."

"Really, what?"

"It's a new song I've written, which we'll be playing. It'll be the third one of the set and it's called *Moving On*..."

"Great, I'll listen out for it," Meg said.

"And," Joe carried on, a little more nervous now, "I wrote it with you in mind. It's about meeting you, how you've changed me, helped me to move on with my life. I guess it's sort of a...

um, love song..." He trailed off, blushing.

Meg stopped, gave a little squeak and threw her arms around his neck. "Really? Oh, Joe, that's fantastic. No one's ever written a song for me before. I'm so excited, I can't wait."

"Well, you'll have to," replied Joe, giving her waist a squeeze as they stood and hugged. "Because it's being kept strictly under wraps until Saturday. For one thing, Ollie hasn't learned all the words yet."

"Aw, Joe, can't you give me a bit of a taster, just a few lines?" pleaded Meg.

Joe was adamant. "No, I want it to be a surprise and for you to hear it at its best. I want you to remember it forever."

"Oh, I will, I'm sure. You're so sweet, Joe! This has got to be the nicest thing anyone's ever done for me." She took his hand and they continued walking blissfully down the road.

CHAPTER 17

●●●●●●●●●●●●●●●●●●●●●●●●●●●●●●●

MAKING PLANS

"Hey, Kez, where's Sonja? I haven't seen her for ages."

Matt lifted his head from the grass he was sprawled on and squinted up into the sunlight, searching for Kerry. She was sitting on a park bench alongside Maya and Cat, eating a Magnum and soaking up the late afternoon sunshine.

Kerry bit off a chunk of dark chocolate from her ice cream and let it melt in her mouth before she answered. It gave her time to prepare her rehearsed line.

"Well, you know that headache she had on the night of your party? It's turned into flu. She's really sick with it."

Kerry hated lying but she knew she had to. No one else must know Sonja's dilemma right now, not even Ollie. Sonja had sworn her to secrecy.

"Poor Son," Matt sympathised. "She must be really hacked off that it's happened at the start of the summer hols. Maybe I ought to go and see how she is. What d'you think, Kerry?"

"I've already put Ollie off doing that. I think she's best left alone for a few days until she's feeling better," Kerry advised. "Anyway, you don't want to catch it before your big weekend, do you?"

Kerry had strict instructions not to let anyone near Sonja's house. Her family had bought the flu line – anyone would, she looked so pale and miserable – and Son was pretty much holed up in her bedroom fretting about what to do with her life and feeling acutely anti-social.

"That's true," Matt observed. "Although a bit of throatiness might help Ollie's vocals. So do you think she'll be able to make it for the festival? She'll be gutted if she misses out."

Kerry shrugged. She had no idea whether or not Sonja was going to Dansby. It was no doubt way down on her list of priorities at the moment.

"I'll give her a ring, see what her plans are," she replied. Keen to get off the subject of Sonja in case she slipped up, Kerry carried on, "So, do we know who's coming and who isn't yet?"

Matt sat up and began counting on his fingers.

"Well, there's me, Ol, Joe, Billy and Andy. We're definites..."

"Obviously," Ollie cut in.

"Then there's, uh... actually, I think that's it for the boys. Hang on, though, what about Nick?"

"Oh, yeah, he's coming for our set," said Ollie. "He's even borrowed a transit from a mate to hump all our gear in. But he can't stay because he's got no one to cover for him at the café on Sunday."

"And what about Alex?" Kerry asked, looking at Maya. "And, more importantly, *you*, Maya? Are you coming?"

Maya smiled. "Yes and no," she said cryptically. "I'm coming, but Alex has decided not to."

"Wow, Maya, that's brilliant," Cat squeaked. Seeing the puzzled look on her friend's face she quickly added, "What I mean *is*, it's a shame about Alex, but fab about you."

"Yeah, great, Maya," Kerry added. "How come your parents changed their minds?"

"They didn't, but I'm going, OK?" said Maya, her chin stuck out in a gesture of defiance. "I'm sick of being treated like a baby while my kid sister gets to do anything she wants. So I'm going to have one last talk with them to get them to see it my way. Then, even if they don't, I'm going."

"Ooh, you're brave," Kerry said. "I don't think I'd have the guts to do that."

"Yes, but your parents aren't being completely unreasonable, nor are they suffering from a bad case of double standards, are they?" explained Maya. "So the bottom line is that I'm coming with you, with or without the senior Joshis' blessing."

"Great." Matt said. "Now, how about the rest of you girls?"

"Well, I've got the day off work at the chemist, and Mum and Dad are OK 'cause they know Ollie'll be there," said Kerry.

"And me and Vikki are definites," Cat added, "though if conditions are *too* grim I might bail out early."

"Wimp!" cried Matt.

"Well, *I* don't know what it's going to be like, I've never been to one of these things before. But if it's a mud-soaked, flea-bitten hell hole there's no way I'm staying." Cat tapped her open-toed sandal petulantly on the tarmac path in front of her and continued filing her already perfect talons.

"Aw, poor liddle girl doesn't want to get dirty, does she?" teased Matt.

"No, I don't," Cat snapped. "And if it's like you say, with cold showers and no privacy, then you can just forget it. I don't share my soap suds with anyone, I'll have you know."

"Actually, Cat," Matt said, "in all seriousness, if you do hate it, you can grab a lift back to the train station with me in the afternoon. I'll be picking Anna up after her shift at the End. Though I bet you'll be having such a great time, you won't want to. If the weather's anything like this, you can always sunbathe in the field somewhere. Just make sure you don't sit in a cow pat."

"Cheers."

"So those are the definite overnighters then?" said Matt, doing a quick calculation on his fingers. "Five boys and five girls, plus Sonja if she's better."

"Don't forget Meg," Joe piped up, colouring slightly. "She's definitely coming. I'm picking her up on the way through."

"Right," Cat said and began counting on her fingers. "That makes six girls, seven if you count Sonja. How's the tent situation coming along, lads?"

Matt and Ollie looked at each other, read each others thoughts and burst out laughing.

"Uh... haven't got round to digging ours out of the garage yet," admitted Matt.

"Um, me neither," Ollie confessed.

"But you're sure you've got tents? I mean,

we're not going to end up sleeping under a tree, are we?" Maya quizzed.

"Nah, don't worry, " said Matt. "It'll be cool. I know exactly where ours is, I saw it the other day when I was rooting in the garage for something else."

"OK. And yours, Ollie?" Maya said, turning to a grinning Ollie on the grass in front of her.

"Uh... pass," he said. "I know it's knocking about somewhere but I'll have to ask my old man where."

"We'll do it tonight, eh, Ol?" urged Kerry. "As soon as we get back."

"Sure."

"So what about the sleeping arrangements then?" Cat piped up. "I mean, no offence here, but the thought of sharing a tent with Matt's sweaty feet stuck in my face all night doesn't appeal somehow."

"I have to agree," replied Matt, his eyes twinkling. "Though in my case it's the prospect of listening to you snoring all night."

Cat was indignant. "I do not snore!"

"How do you know," Matt asked, "if you're asleep?"

"I just know, OK."

"What, one of your conquests has told you, has he?" Matt continued, enjoying watching Cat squirm. He put on an affected voice. "No, darling, you don't snore. Or pass wind in the night. You're simply perfect, my love..."

Cat shot Kerry a conspiratorial look and they both sniggered. Once again someone was making way off the mark assumptions about Cat's love-life.

"Look," Cat insisted, "the reason I know I don't snore is because I've taped myself asleep, all right?"

The others turned to look at her to see if she was joking. She wasn't.

"*What?*" giggled Maya.

"Well, why not?" Cat frowned. "I wanted to know, so I put a cassette on our old portable and taped myself one night. And you know what? I never made a sound."

"She probably forgot to press *Record*," chuckled Matt.

Cat shot him a killer glance and prepared for her next dig.

"Anyway, Matt, I don't particularly want to share a tent with you and Anna, either," she sneered. "The thought of you two being all loved up together makes my stomach turn."

"Ooh, I hadn't thought of that," Maya joined in, her nose wrinkling. "What with Matt and Anna, and Kerry and Ollie, and Joe and Meg, I think maybe we should have one tent for the lovebirds and one for those of us who want a decent night's sleep."

"Wouldn't it be simpler if we put the girls in one and the boys in the other?" suggested Joe, anxious not to get into a compromising situation with Meg so soon in their relationship. "That way," he added, "there'll be no potentially embarrassing moments."

"Boring!" cried Matt. "That doesn't sound like any fun at all."

"But practical," Kerry added. "I agree with Joe – that's by far the best idea. What d'you say, Maya?"

"Yep, I go along with that."

"That's settled then," said Cat. "And if pervy old Matt doesn't like it, he'll have to go and get his kicks elsewhere!"

CHAPTER 18

● ●

TIME TO TALK

Owen checked out of his hotel in the city and headed for the railway station and a train that would take him back to Winstead. As he walked along the road he took his mobile out of his jacket pocket and checked it for the hundredth time since he'd arrived. No messages. It was Wednesday and Sonja still hadn't returned his call from Sunday. Owen wasn't exactly surprised.

When he stepped off the train at Winstead Station forty minutes later, he scurried furtively out of the exit and hurried towards Sonja's house. He didn't want anyone to see him, especially Anna. By rights he should now be on a train home to Newcastle.

But Owen couldn't go home, not without seeing Sonja first. As expected, his course had been so intensive there hadn't been a chance to ring from the hotel – at least, not at a sociable hour. And anyway, he'd avoided that. There were some things you just couldn't sort out over the phone, he'd decided. So here he was, on a little detour; one which he hoped would go some way to making amends.

It was teatime when he arrived at the Harveys'. When he got to the door he stopped for a second and took a deep breath. Then, his heart in his mouth and his hands damp with sweat, he pressed the bell and waited. Moments later the door opened and Sonja's dad stood in front of him.

"Hello, Owen," he said cheerily. "What a surprise. Come in."

Owen stepped into the house and stood edgily in the hallway.

"Sonja didn't say you were coming..."

"No, it's kind of a surprise."

"Oh. Well, you're lucky," he carried on. "She's had a dose of awful flu that seems to be going round. Fortunately, I think she's on the mend now. Mind you, I'm guessing. We've hardly seen her – she's been holed up in that bedroom like a hermit. *Sonja*! Someone to see you..."

He gave Owen a wink. "I'll let you surprise her."

"Thanks, Mr Harvey."

Owen stood, his gaze transfixed on the stairs,

listening to Sonja's bedroom door open, staring as first her feet then her legs and finally the rest of her trudged down the stairs towards him in her dressing gown and slippers. She didn't look up until she was near the bottom, but when she saw him, her vacant expression turned to a cold stare.

"What are you doing here?" she hissed, her voice lowered so the rest of the family wouldn't hear.

"Sonja, I had to see you," Owen said in a low voice back. "I couldn't go home without sorting this out."

She shot a look around the hall and to the doors leading off it.

"Not here!' she instructed. "Hang on... *Dad!* Owen and I are just going up to my room, OK?"

"OK, love!"

On hearing his name mentioned, Mrs Harvey strolled out of the kitchen. "Owen! I didn't know you were coming. You didn't tell us, Sonja," she said, looking quizzically at her daughter.

"I didn't know, Mum."

"Oh, I see. Well, will you be staying for something to eat?" Sonja's mum asked innocently.

Sonja cringed. *For God's sake say no*, she thought, dreading the idea of them sitting around the kitchen table playing happy families.

"Uh, no thanks, Mrs Harvey. I've got to get back to Newcastle tonight. Another time perhaps?"

Not on your life, thought Sonja bitterly.

"Of course. Perhaps next time you're down," said Mrs Harvey, heading back to the kitchen.

They made their way upstairs to Sonja's room. She closed the door behind them then sat on the edge of her bed, her arms folded defensively across her chest. Owen stood nervously in front of her.

"So what do you want?" she demanded unsmilingly.

Owen took a deep breath. "To say I'm sorry," he said simply.

"For what? For speaking your mind? For telling me what you think and letting me know what you're *really* like?"

Owen opened his mouth to answer but was cut short by Sonja's vicious tones.

"Why apologise? I should be thanking you for giving me such a great insight into your character. I could have been living with you before I found out what an insensitive, unsupportive jerk you are. Now, fortunately, I don't have to. You know the way out – close the door when you leave," she finished dismissively and turned away to pick up the book she'd been reading.

"I know, you're right, I deserve whatever you throw at me," sighed Owen. "But I was so shell-shocked when you told me, the wires in my brain got crossed. I reacted badly and for that I'm so sorry. That person you sat opposite in the Plaza wasn't the real me. It was a little boy, scared witless, who suddenly felt like he was in too deep. I panicked."

"How do you think *I've* felt this last week?" Sonja replied. "It hasn't exactly been a party for me."

"I know, and that's the other thing I feel terrible about," Owen told her. "On Sunday I was only thinking of me, I didn't consider what *you* must be going through at all. You must have gone to hell and back since you found out, and I bet you were expecting me to be there for you, to help you get through it."

"I wasn't *expecting* anything," fibbed Sonja, keen not to let him see just how much she *had* been expecting. "But I was *hoping* you might be there for me..."

"...And I wasn't. I'll never forgive myself for being so selfish. It was pathetic."

"Yep," Sonja agreed, though she felt herself beginning to thaw a little. "Although I was so uptight, I didn't give you much of a chance to explain yourself."

"That was understandable. You must be under so much strain and I didn't help much. I only hope that at some point you might be able to forgive me," Owen said wearily. "And in spite of the rubbish I came out with on Sunday, I want you to know that I *will* support you, whatever happens, and I hope we can work something out."

Sonja felt a huge wave of relief course through her body as a weight lifted from her. Knowing that Owen was willing to help her get through this rotten mess was a great comfort.

"Thanks. I don't think I can cope on my own," she found herself saying. "It's too big a thing. Only Kerry knows – she's been brilliant. But it's not down to her. This is my life..."

"...*Our* lives," Owen corrected her. "I'd hate to lose you, Son. You're the best thing that's ever happened to me, I mean that. Don't let's break up."

Neither said anything for a few moments. When Sonja finally spoke, her voice was small but quite firm.

"Well, if you really want to be there for me," she said, "you could come with me to the Family Planning Clinic when I've made an appointment. I– I don't know exactly what I'm going to do yet, but I think I'd like to have your support."

Owen took a few strides towards Sonja, sat on the edge of the bed and wrapped his arms around her. "'Course I will," he murmured.

"And, uh, while I don't want to put any more pressure on you," he carried on after a few moments' silence, "did you mean it when you said you weren't sure if you wanted us to live together?"

"Do *you* still want us to live together. After all this?"

"Of course."

"Then we will."

"That's great," smiled Owen, kissing the top of her head. "And look, we will get through this. Together."

CHAPTER 19

● ●

MATT TO THE RESCUE

"Boy, do I feel grateful to be alive."

Cat climbed gingerly out of Joe's Fiat, stretched elaborately, then lent a hand to drag first Vikki, then Billy, off the back seat and into the fresh air.

"Gee, now I know how it feels to be one baked bean too many in a Heinz can," Vikki commented. "It was a bit tight on space in the back. I knew I should have beaten Meg to the front seat," she added, casting a glance at Joe's girlfriend who had by now leapt agilely out from the passenger side door.

"I don't think the driver would have been too pleased," said Cat as she watched Joe looking doe-eyed at Meg. She'd seen him casting longing looks at his girlfriend on several occasions as he'd driven to Dansby from Winstead. "Hey, you nearly hit fifty miles an hour on the dual carriageway, Joe," she carried on. "For a minute, I thought I'd got into Michael Schumacher's car by mistake. "

"Ha *ha*," said Joe. "You could have gone with Matt. I nearly lost sight of him a couple of times, even though I had my foot to the floor most of the way here."

"Yeah, and I was doing all of fifty-five," Matt grinned. "I didn't dare go any quicker in case a door fell off."

"At least we're here now," said Kerry.

"Hmmm," Cat looked around. "*Here,* as in a field miles from anywhere. Are you sure you've got the right place, boys?"

"It'll get busier. It's only because we had to get here early," Ollie explained, jumping down from the passenger seat of the battered blue Transit Nick had borrowed for the occasion.

"You girls wait," Nick added. "In a couple of hours this site will be teeming with gorgeous young men for you to lech at. By the time you get back to your tents tonight there won't be room to move. And if I might make a suggestion," he added, "if you boys park your cars over there, so that you've got the hedge at one end and that tree at the other, you'll see that you've made a sort of boxy area to erect your tents in. That way, you'll give yourselves a lot more space that can't be pinched by other campers."

"There speaks one with several decades of festival experience under his ever-increasing belt," Ollie chuckled, patting his uncle on the stomach over-hanging his jeans, and watching as Joe and Matt manoeuvred their vehicles in the way Nick had suggested.

"So, Maya," Cat carried on, her eyes glinting. "I've been dying to know how you got on with your parents. Are you here with their blessing or have you had to fabricate some fabulous lie to explain your absence? We had a bet in the car – Joe and Meg reckon you wrapped your parents round your little finger, while me, Vikki and Billy prefer to think of you as a fugitive. What's the story?"

Maya giggled. "This lot have already heard," she said, referring to her car companions, "but for the rest of you, here goes..." She related the story which had unfolded the previous evening.

"Y'know it's the Dansby festival tomorrow?" Maya had said to her parents.

"Hmmm?" her father had replied. "What about it?"

"I want to camp overnight with the others."

Her father had looked up from his newspaper. "You know the answer is no, Maya."

"Why don't you trust me?"

"We do," Nina said.

"Then why don't you prove it? Or you might find I just go off and do what I want anyway."

Her mother had laughed. "Don't be silly, Maya, you're far too sensible for that."

This had riled Maya. "If I'm so sensible, why the heck won't you let me stay overnight? It's not as though I'm going to come back in a drug-fuelled state or with tattoos all up my arm, is it?" she'd raged.

"Don't raise your voice to your mother, Maya," said Sanjay, "or you won't be going to the festival at all."

Maya had been so angry something inside her snapped. She was sick to death of being reasonable with her parents. She'd had enough.

"There's no point discussing this any more," she had said calmly. "But just to let you know, I *am* going to Dansby, I *will* be staying the night and there's *nothing* you can do about it."

"Maya, that's brilliant," Vikki cut in. "Good for you. Wow, if it had been me saying all that, my mum would have locked me in a cupboard for the weekend! It's OK," she added to a startled-looking Meg, "I'm joking but, well, you know what I mean. So what happened next? Did they forbid you to leave the house?"

"Thankfully, it didn't come to that," Maya continued. "I stormed off to my room and Dad rang Joe's mum – they're quite chummy, what with her working at the surgery. And because she was OK about Joe going, and kept going on about how responsible I was, they had a rethink, ordered me back down to the kitchen and said I could go after all. So long as I brought this..." She pulled a mobile phone from her pocket. "...and promised to ring in the morning to let them know everything's all right."

"So you won't be getting your hair dyed pink or having an eyebrow pierced while you're here then?" Andy joked.

"Ooh, do they do things like that?" asked Cat, suddenly more interested in her surroundings. "I'd like to watch a few people having it done, see them squirm a bit. *Purely* for professional reasons, of course," she added quickly, seeing a few startled faces around her.

"And on *that* sick note, I think we ought to go and sort out this soundcheck," Ollie chuckled, looking at his watch. He delved into the front pocket of his combats, drew out the backstage passes and handed them round to the boys and Nick.

"And in the mean time you girlies can have some fun putting the tents up," Matt sniggered, lobbing his car keys at Vikki.

"No problem," she replied, turning to her friends and grimacing. "Let's get started."

As the boys all piled into the back of the transit to head off towards the stage, the girls began dragging tent equipment from the boots of the cars.

Kerry and Sonja hung back a little.

"How are you feeling?" asked Kerry in a low voice.

"Ooh, miserable, tearful, like I shouldn't have come. How's that for starters?" Sonja replied, a forced smile on her face.

"Don't you feel any better now you and Owen are sorted?"

"In a lot of ways, yes. At least we're going to the clinic next week. But it still doesn't make it go away. The bottom line is that I'm still pregnant and I still don't know what to do about it."

"I know," Kerry said, looking crestfallen. "I'm sorry."

"Hey, it's not your fault. I feel awful for dragging you into this."

Sonja forced herself to lighten up. "I'll be OK once we get to see some bands," she said. "I'll get my bopping hat on and we'll be well away. It'll make a change from staring at the four walls of my bedroom."

She gave Kerry's arm a little squeeze and

smiled, even though inside she wasn't laughing.

"Why are we doing this?" Cat queried five minutes and several tent poles and bits of rope later.

"To show them that we're not idiots," said Vikki, "and that we can in fact put up a couple of mangy old tents."

"Yeah," Maya agreed. "And you can bet they think we're going to totally mess up."

"OK, so why not look at it like this?" said Cat, chucking her pole on the ground and stripping off her shorts and top to reveal a skimpy bikini. She took a beach towel out of her bag, laid it on the grass, sat down and began rubbing Factor 8 sunscreen all over her bare bits.

"If we're really savvy," she carried on, "and if we want to play them at their own game, surely the thing to do is not rise to the challenge? What *I* propose is that we all have a lie down, catch some morning rays and leave the hard work to *them* when they get back."

"You know, Cat," said Maya, "sometimes I think you've got a brain the size of a planet."

With that, she unbuttoned her top ready to do the same.

● ● ●

When the boys drove round to the back of the stage, they found more people rushing around there than at the front. Parking up as near to the platform as possible, they leapt out of the van and watched as Nick hurried off to find an organiser. The others began milling about, soaking up the atmosphere, feeling increasingly pumped up to be even a small part of it.

"I feel nervous already," said Joe, his face a couple of shades paler than normal.

"I know what you mean." Billy replied. "It's a mixture of nerves and anticipation and excitement. I bet even the biggest names feel like this before a gig."

"'Cept they already know what to expect," Joe added.

"So do we," reasoned Ollie. "It'll just be like the Railway Tavern, only bigger and better. We'll be fine. It's going to be brilliant."

"Hey, look over there, I'm sure that's Deke." Matt pointed to a lone figure in the distance, mobile phone clamped to his ear. "I'll just go and say hi. Catch up with you lot later."

Matt got close enough to speak to Deke just as he finished his call.

"Hey, Deke. How are you doing, mate?"

"Uh, pretty stressed, man," Deke replied, rubbing the back of his neck with his free hand.

"One of the guys I booked has gone AWOL and I haven't been able to get anyone else at such short notice. I guess I'll have to double up with the first act I've got on."

Matt's brain went into overdrive. "What d'you want to do that for, when I could fill in for you?" he demanded.

"Huh?" Deke didn't cotton on for a few seconds.

"Come on, mate, give me a chance," Matt cajoled. "All I need is a stack of tracks to go through. You can vet my choice if you like. Then you just need to point me in the direction of the decks and I'll be away. You can't lose."

Deke scratched his designer stubble for a while, letting Matt's suggestion sink in. "Uh, yeah," he said finally. "Why not? You had some pretty good stuff at that party of yours the other night... let's give it a shot."

Matt felt he was going to explode with joy. "Oh, wow, man, that's great!" he said, slapping Deke on the back. "Thanks a lot."

Deke laughed. "No worries, just don't let me down. Meet me over there in an hour?" He pointed to a bank of speakers at one end of the stage. "You'll be on fairly promptly after the start, so I'll show you where everything is and you can begin setting up."

Matt charged back to the lads to tell them what was happening.

"Matt, that's brilliant!" they chorused amid a lot of arm-punching and back-slapping.

"This is gonna be *such* a brilliant day for us all," Ollie raved. "It's like it was meant to be. Hey, Nick," he called, seeing his uncle rushing towards them with various bits of paper flapping in his hand, "Matt's gigging here too!"

"Matt, that's great. Good for you," Nick smiled. Then his face dropped and he took on a more serious manner. "Now – can we all get our backsides in gear, please? Only I've just spoken to one of the organisers and if we don't get on-stage in the next ten minutes, we're going to miss our soundcheck."

• • •

"Only a few seconds to go, girls."

Cat and the others stood at the front of the festival site and craned their necks to see what was going on. Ever since Ollie had rushed round to tell them about Matt's brilliant opportunity, they had been checking their watches, getting more excited with every passing moment.

As the opening act finished their set and retreated to the wings, a few seconds' silence was suddenly broken by the intro to Artful Dodger's *Re-rewind*. The girls studied the DJ console to one side of the stage and Cat ear-blastingly gave out a little squeal.

"There he is!"

Sure enough, there was Matt – or at least, the top of his head, bobbing up and down to the track he'd just put on. All around him, guys were on the stage, getting it ready for the next live act. There were plenty of distractions, cables being rolled out, pieces of equipment being pushed back and forth.

And in the midst of it all Matt was looking right at home, like he been doing this kind of thing all his life.

"He's brilliant," enthused Maya, grinning broadly and and snapping away madly with the camera she'd naturally brought. She turned to see what the growing crowd was up to and began frantically taking more pictures of them as well.

"Look, they're totally rockin'," she squealed to the others, who turned to see a mass of heads moving up and down, appreciating the music Matt was playing.

"God, he'll be impossible after this," Cat complained fondly. "His head's big enough as it is. He'll need a train to carry it home by the time he's finished."

She smiled, proud of the fact that it was her friend up there, then carried on bopping and cheering like she was in the front row of the best gig of her life.

CHAPTER 20

• •

RESULT!

"I need the loo."

Kerry looked wildly around as they stood waiting for The Loud to come on.

"Me too," Sonja added, "sort of, quite desperately. Ooh look – there's a Portakabin thing way over there. That looks promising. Catch you guys later."

Sonja grabbed Kerry and headed for the temporary toilets, while the others carried on watching the band playing up on-stage.

"Phew, I'm busting," said Kerry, leaping up the three rickety stairs and opening the door marked 'Women'. "And, they're not too bad at the moment," she added, looking around before disappearing into one of the cubicles.

"Yeah, imagine how grim they'll be by the end

of the night," commented Sonja next door.

"Ugh, I know. Hey, this one flushes as well. Result."

Kerry came out and stood at the sink to wash her hands.

"*Omigod*, I don't believe it," she heard Sonja shriek.

"What? What is it?" Kerry rushed over to the door to hear what sounded like Sonja weeping from the other side.

"Sonja, are you OK?" she said, pushing the door with her hand to try and get in.

"I'm f-f-fine," Sonja stuttered from behind the door. "I, uh..."

She broke off to unlock the door and peep out at Kerry.

"I um... just wondered if you'd got any tampons...?"

"What? You mean...? You've got your... You're not...?" Kerry's hand flew to her mouth and her eyes lit up like beacons.

"Not pregnant." A beaming Sonja opened the door fully and leapt into the arms of her friend.

"Oh, wow, I can't believe it!" Sonja cried, tears of relief streaming down her face.

"Me neither." Kerry hugged her, patting her on the back over and over again.

"What a relief!"

"I *know!*" Kerry stood back to study the huge smile on Sonja's face. She looked a lifetime younger than she had five minutes ago.

Sonja wiped the tears from her eyes. "Isn't it just the best news?"

"It's the very best."

"I must tell Owen."

"You know his mobile number, don't you?" Kerry asked as they ran out into the lovely warm sunshine.

"Yeah, I'll borrow Cat's phone and give him a call. He'll be *so* relieved."

"I wonder why you were so late then?" pondered Kerry as they made their way back to the others.

"Who knows? I guess it could have been all the worry of my exams. And I reckon that half the reason I've felt so rotten and weepy and miserable these last few days is because I've had PMS. No wonder I was feeling bloated and had sore boobs. But I was so convinced I was pregnant I didn't recognise the symptoms."

"What a nightmare," Kerry sighed. "I'm so pleased it's all over."

"I wonder if any of the others have got tampons?" wondered Sonja as they caught sight of Cat, Maya, Meg and Vikki giving it loads in front of them.

"Someone's bound to. Hey, you lot!" Kerry called from a metre or so away.

"Shhh, don't shout," hissed Sonja.

"Sonja, give me some credit," Kerry tutted. "I was only trying to get their attention."

"What's up?" asked Vikki, dancing over to them.

"I'm after tampons," Sonja said.

"Sorry, can't help you," Vikki replied. "Hey!" she called to the others in a booming voice. "Son wants some tampons. You guys got any?"

As Cat, Meg and Maya began rifling through their bags, Kerry and Sonja cracked up and hid behind their hands.

"You can get tofu burgers and chips over there," they heard a cackling lad call from behind. "Dunno about tampons though."

"Oh, no, I'm going to die of embarrassment," wailed Kerry.

"Here you go," Cat beamed, shoving something into Sonja's hand. "It was rolling around in the bottom of my bag. It's the only one though."

"Cheers, Cat. I guess I could ask Matt to get me some when he goes to pick Anna up."

"He'll love you for that," Kerry laughed.

"It'll do him good," chuckled Sonja. "It'll help him get in touch with his feminine side... Hey,

Cat, can I borrow your mobile for a minute?"

"Sure." Cat took her phone from her bag and tossed it to Sonja who disappeared off to find a quiet spot to make that call to Owen.

Her hands shook as she punched in his number.

"Hello...?"

"Owen, it's me!" Sonja shouted above the noise of the track being played up on-stage, the excitement in her voice still obvious. "I had to call you. I've got the most brilliant news..."

"Go on," Owen replied, hardly daring to think what she might say.

"I'm not pregnant!" Sonja shouted. "It was a false alarm. Isn't that brilliant?"

"Oh, Son, that's great!" he said. "God, what a relief."

"I know. I can hardly believe it myself. I only just found out."

"You're at Dansby, right?"

"Yeah and me and Kerry were in the loo and..." Sonja broke off, aware that the music had stopped and that her shouting could probably be heard by anyone within a five-kilometre radius. She burst out laughing.

"Actually, Owen," she said more quietly, "you don't need to hear all this now. Look, The Loud are about to go on. I'll call you when I get home, OK?"

"Sure. Son. You're OK, are you?"

"Never felt better. Catch you later."

"Sure. I love you."

"Me too. Bye."

Sonja hurried back to the others, a massive grin plastered all over her face. When she got near, she noticed Kerry standing at the front of the crowd looking like she was about to be sick, while the rest of her group hollered and whooped for all they were worth. Looking up, Sonja could see Ollie, Joe, Billy and Andy just about to begin their set. Sonja joined in, rushing to the front and shouting like her life depended on it.

Up on the stage Ollie was in his own world – everything other than the music he and his three friends were making was shut out. He was vaguely aware that he was standing two metres up on a big stage, looking out on to a sunlit afternoon. Several hundred expectant faces were staring up at him from the middle of a vast field of greenish-brown grass.

But it was the weirdest sensation – he almost felt like he was having an out-of-body experience and looking down on someone else singing his songs. He was concentrating so hard, he wouldn't have noticed if a UFO had landed in front of him.

But they were good.

"No, they're not just good, they're bloody brilliant," Cat yelled to a guy nearby who was commentating to some mates while the boys played their set.

"Ollie's just a complete love god up there, isn't he?" Kerry swooned.

"Come on, they all are," giggled Sonja. She was on a high now and nothing could dampen her spirits.

As they finished the song, Ollie bowed to the enthusiastic cheers from the crowd and spoke into the mike.

"This is a new song, written by our drummer and my best mate, Joe Gladwin," he announced, turning to Joe and grinning.

Joe was taken aback; he hadn't expected this. But he was dead chuffed too and gave his friend the thumbs up as they began the intro to *Moving On*.

In the audience Meg turned to the others, her face alight with happiness. "This is the one he wrote for me," she called to the girls, her excitement obvious. "Ooh, I must shut up and listen to the words..."

"I didn't know Joe wrote songs," Sonja observed.

"Me neither," said Kerry, "but will you listen to it? It's absolutely beautiful. Meg must be made up that he's written it specially for her."

They listened in silence to the haunting ballad. At the end, the reaction from the crowd was ecstatic and, behind his drums, Joe felt himself grow a little taller as pride surged through his body.

"I wonder if anything will come of this weekend?" Kerry sighed to Sonja as the band began their next song.

"Bound to," her friend replied. "You mark my words, Kez, if they carry on being as good as this, they're on their way."

• • •

"Sorry I'm a bit late. It's been an amazing afternoon. I got here as fast as I could."

Anna smiled and gave Matt a kiss on the cheek. "How did it go?" she asked, climbing into the car and grateful to take the weight off her feet.

"Brilliant. The Loud went down a storm. But what's even better – and I'm so gutted that you missed this – was that *I* played on-stage before them."

"*What?*" Anna was taken aback. "How d'you mean?"

"Well, remember my mate, Deke? He was let down by a DJ so I took his place. It was the most awesome experience, Anna. I'll never forget it."

"Matt, that's great," she said, running her hand through his hair as they pulled away from the station. "I *wish* I hadn't had to work. I can't believe I wasn't there."

"I know. But don't worry – you can come next time."

"What, you mean they've booked you for something else?"

"Er, *no*, not exactly. But two other promoters came up to me afterwards, gave me their cards and took my number. Which was even more fab. Honestly, I've got a great vibe about this, Anna. I reckon things could start to happen from now on."

"Wow, that's brilliant!" enthused Anna. "I'm so mad I missed it. Still, I'll make sure I'm there when one of these promoter guys books you for thousands of pounds and a free limo for the evening thrown in."

"Well, there's nothing like getting too carried away, is there? " Matt laughed. "Oh, God – I nearly forgot!"

Matt put on the brakes, swerved across the road and screeched into the lay-by in front of a row of shops.

Anna grabbed hold of the sides of her seat and shouted, "Crikey, Matt, you nearly gave me a heart attack. What are you doing?"

"I've just remembered," came the cool reply, "I
need to get something for Sonja..."

CHAPTER 21

• •

CARRY ON CAMPING

"Look, there they are!" Cat cried, pointing and
jumping up and down with excitement. With
Vikki at her side, she ran full tilt at Ollie, Joe,
Andy and Billy as they returned from nosing
around back stage for the third time since they'd
finished their set earlier in the afternoon. The
boys couldn't resist hanging out back there,
soaking up the atmosphere, enjoying being a part
of it all. And, of course, they loved flashing their
passes whenever anyone tried to bar their way
into a no-go area.

The crowd had thickened considerably by now
and the boys had to weave their way through to
the meeting point the gang had agreed on earlier
in the day. When they were within a few metres,
and were spotted by their friends, they were

stopped in their tracks by the sight of Cat and Vikki launching themselves at them like cruise missiles.

"Oh, Ollie!" screamed Cat, waving a piece of paper. "Can I have your autograph, please?"

"And can I have a kiss too, please, Andy!" Vikki hollered.

"OK, OK, don't take the mick," Ollie laughingly shouted above the shrieking and yelling.

"But you're so fab and we love you *sooo* much. Especially you, Joe," howled Cat, throwing herself on her friend and pretending to rip off his black, long-sleeved T-shirt. "Can't you write a song about me too, *pleeeease*?"

The others in the gang were creased up at Vikki and Cat's over-the-top antics, even more so because the lads looked increasingly embarrassed by it. This, of course, made the pair even worse.

As the warm afternoon turned into a muggy evening, the gang partied like it was the last night of their lives. The whole atmosphere was of one big rave. Everyone was friendly. The gang danced manically, rushing between the two stages so they could catch their specific acts, sometimes splitting up into two groups, always returning to their chosen meeting point so they didn't lose each other.

Fascinated by what was going on at the fringes, Cat, Maya, Andy and Vikki spent some time wandering around the makeshift stalls people had set up, selling everything from Jewish latka potato cakes to dodgy-looking pipes to organic underwear.

"I quite fancy getting my head shaved," Vikki observed at one point as they watched a body artist painting an intricate picture on a bald man's head. "What do you think?"

"I think you'd regret it in the morning, hon," Cat whispered, giggling at the thought. She suddenly raised her head and sniffed the air. "Mmm, something smells good. Shall we get something to eat, I'm starving?"

Cat dragged her friends to where the smell was coming from, then pulled a face as she looked into the cauldron of steaming food.

"Eurrgh, I can't stomach that – it looks like mushy peas," she said with some distaste and hurried away.

By the time the last act finished and the gang trooped exhausted back to their bagged area, the girls were sorely regretting not having put the tents up. Now the vast field was crammed with tents, camper vans and caravans of all shapes and sizes.

"It's like being in a commune," Cat remarked

as she picked her way between them, Ollie's powerful torch showing the way.

"And, of course, we've got the only spot on the site which doesn't have any sleeping quarters – yet," announced Matt with some amusement. They looked at their bare little patch of ground which seemed to have shrunk from earlier in the day.

"Don't worry," Joe said, fishing out his car keys and opening the boot. "It won't take long to put these two tents up."

He began hauling their camping equipment out of the car, passing it to Matt and Ollie, who started trying to sort out which bits belonged where.

"I'll put some coffee on," said Cat, desperate not to get involved. She grabbed the portable gas ring instead and wondered how on earth it was supposed to work.

"Hey, yours seems heaps bigger than mine," Matt said as he pulled his tent from the bag and began unrolling it.

"Well, it's supposed to sleep six," said Ollie.

"Yeah, so's mine – but it seems a lot smaller. Maybe it's shrunk in the rain over the years. Shall we get yours up first?"

Everyone mucked in and set to work on Ollie's tent – everyone, that is, except Cat who had given up on the gas ring and was now rifling through various bags looking for plastic cups.

"Wow, that looks great," she said when the tent was finally up. "It's much roomier than I was expecting. But where are the rest of you going to sleep?"

"Very funny. Actually," said Matt, "didn't we tell you, Cat? You're in the back of Joe's Fiat for the night."

"Marvellous. Who with?" she shot back.

"Uh, OK," Ollie commanded. "Can we make a start on Matt's now, please?"

He grabbed one end and passed the other to Andy.

"Pooh, it's a bit stinky, Matt," commented Andy, wrinkling his nose distastefully. "How old is it?"

"Oh, ancient. I should think we only used it once or twice."

"Matt, it's as rotten as a pear," Ollie said as he slipped a pole in the side and watched it come out along the seam at the top. "And, for goodness' sake, it's *tiny*."

"I *thought* it was..."

Matt suddenly clapped his hand to his face and went horribly quiet.

"OK, Matt, what is it you're not telling us here?" asked Maya.

"I've brought the wrong one," he wailed. "That's the small one – the really old one we meant to throw out years ago..."

"I can see why. It's blinking useless." Ollie slipped another pole into a seam, pulled it taut by setting his weight against Billy at the other end and waited.

Rrrrriiiiiiiip!

Seconds later, Ollie tumbled on to the grass as the tent practically tore in half.

"Ah, yes," said Matt sagely. "I remember now. The other tent's in the attic – so it wouldn't go rotten. Sorry, guys."

"Are you sure you didn't do this on purpose?" Sonja asked. "I wouldn't put it past you to pull a trick like this just for the hell of it."

"I swear... I mean, do you honestly think I'd want to spend the night sharing a tent with seven stunning girlies... and four smelly, hairy guys?" Matt's face broke out into a grin.

"Well, you know what's going to happen now, don't you?" Sonja carried on. "We're going to have to fight over who's sleeping in the cars."

"Bagsy the Fiat," screeched Billy before anyone else could even draw breath.

"And I'll have Matt's old banger," Andy yelled.

"So that leaves me, Ol and Joe squeezing in the tent with the girls. Which by my reckoning..."

Matt stopped for a moment to count on his fingers "...means you get two girls each. And I get three – sorry, Anna! What do you say, lads? Are you up for it?"

"No, are *you* up for it, baby?" Vikki roared, striding up to Matt and engulfing him in an enormous bear hug.

"Uh, well, actually," Matt squeaked, his voice suddenly two octaves higher, "I'm not at all sure that I am."

"Didn't think so," she said, dropping him like a stone and watching him crumple in a heap on the grass.

"Well, I'm too worn out to argue," said Anna. "So it doesn't matter to me who I sleep with because I won't notice. I'll be dead to the world as soon as I shut my eyes."

"Hmmm, me too," Kerry yawned.

"Wow, what a lot of party animals you all are," Matt observed. He looked around him. "Talking of which, where's the biggest party animal of them all?"

"She was making coffee, I think," said Maya and turned to peer into Ollie's tent. "Oy, you lot," she called. "Over here."

They gathered around the entrance to the tent. There, sprawled in the middle of it, was Cat, sound asleep and snoring loudly.

Matt put his finger to his mouth to quieten everyone, then whispered, "On the count of three."

"One. Two. Three...!"

"Arrrrrrgh!" they bellowed as, with one spring, they all leaped into the tent.

Sugar

SECRETS...

...& Sunburn

SNEAK PREVIEW!

"The sun..." Catrina Osgood murmured dreamily.

She stared out of the big bay window of the End-of-the-Line caf..., where the hovering rain clouds made the so-called summer sky seem almost as grey as the pavement. Along with Maya Joshi and Sonja Harvey, she was whiling away a Friday morning, drooling with envy at the holiday their two friends were about to embark on that same day.

"The sea..." Maya chipped in, equally dreamily.

"Stuff the sea!" Cat suddenly brayed, staring across the window-seat table at her friend. "What's the sea got to do with anything?"

"You know – it's the wet stuff that starts where the sand stops," her cousin Sonja said sarcastically. "And when you're on holiday, you go in it and swim and have what's called *fun*."

"Total waste of time, if you ask me," sniffed Cat. "Using up all those valuable sunbathing minutes..."

"Hey, Cat, haven't you heard about that thing with the hole in it?" Maya asked, leaning back on the red banquette and folding her arms.

"*What* thing with the hole in it?" Cat frowned.

"The ozone layer. That's spelt O-Z-O-N-E," Maya teased her.

"Yeah, *yeah*," shrugged Cat, flopping her elbows on to the Formica table top. She knew when she was being made fun of.

"Mmm and the hole in this Ôozone layer'," Sonja joined in, making quote marks in the air with her fingers, "can cause a thing called 'skin cancer'. That's spelt S-K-I-N C-A-N—"

"Enough with the lectures," snorted Cat impatiently.

"Well, there's more to holidays than just lying on a beach frying like a chip!"

"Oh, is that right, Sonja? Well, thank you for telling me. I suppose sunbathing's too relaxed for you. I bet if it was *you* in Ibiza, instead of Kerry and Ollie, you'd spend your whole day playing volleyball or paragliding, or playing volleyball *while* you were paragliding..."

"Para-ball! Volley-gliding! Whatever – it sounds good to me!" grinned Sonja.

"And what about you?" said Cat, pointing an accusing finger at Maya. "If you were in Ibiza, I bet you'd want to be off photographing historical ruins and looking at ancient relics, wouldn't you?"

"No. That's the sort of stuff I do with my parents. And, just for once, I'd like to be on a beach towel next to you, Cat, doing nothing more energetic than listening to my Walkman and lazing in the sun."

Sonja and Cat were both stumped. That wasn't a very Maya-thing to say at all. Lazing wasn't something that came very naturally to the hard-working, earnest Maya Joshi.

"Covered in SPF 20, of course," Maya added with a grin. Even in her fantasies, Maya still had to do the right thing.

"So, Maya," said Cat, narrowing her eyes, "when you're lying on the beach, drowning in factor 20, do you think you'd have enough energy to check out some of the beautiful, bronzed boys strolling past?"

"Excuse *me*!" said Maya, raising her eyebrows in mock outrage. "I am a happily er... dating girl! You'd never catch me ogling boys on the beach!"

"Oooh, pardon me, Miss Goody-Two-Shoes!" said Cat wide-eyed. "Anyway, I only *said* look. You can have a boyfriend and still check out other blokes, you know. It's not against the law. Is it, Son?"

Sonja hesitated for a second and then nodded her head in agreement. It always took her by surprise when she saw things from the same point of view as her cousin. They'd spent so many years bickering as they grew up together that it had almost become second nature.

"Well, I love Owen," she shrugged, "but that doesn't mean I don't sneak the occasional peek at a good-looking bloke. It's only natural, isn't it?"

"What do *you* think, Anna?" Cat bellowed as Anna Michaels walked past after serving another table.

"What about?" asked Anna, using the moment to put her empty tray down and readjust the scrunchie that was working loose from her brown ponytail.

"If you were on holiday with Matt," Cat began, "would you still check out the totty on the beach?"

"There's no harm looking as long as you don't touch!" Anna smiled. "But if you got on to this subject because of Kerry and Ollie going off today, then I'd have to say, with those two, neither of them will be looking at *anybody* else..."

The other girls nodded. Ollie and Kerry had been going out for just over a year now, but were still sickeningly in love with each other.

"That's 'cause this holiday is so, y'know, *special* to them!" Cat grinned mischievously.

"Because it's their first holiday together?" Maya frowned, either oblivious to Cat's meaning or trying her hardest to ignore it.

"Oh, it's their first time for *something* all right!" giggled Cat.

"Mmm, big step for Kez..." muttered Sonja, remembering past conversations with her best friend, when Kerry had told her how she hadn't felt ready for sex, even though she was very sure of her relationship with Ollie.

Sonja felt a wave of guilt; she'd been so caught up in her own traumas lately, she hadn't thought to ask Kerry how she was feeling about the holiday and, well, *everything*.

"Do you really think it'll happen? That they'll sleep together while they're on holiday?" Maya asked, looking around the table at her friends' faces.

"Come on, Maya!" snorted Cat. "Going somewhere hot and romantic with your long-term boyfriend, with not a parent in sight and one bedroom? What do *you* think?"

For a second, all four girls were silent, lost in their own private thoughts.

What do I think? pondered Maya, gazing blankly up at the cloudy sky outside. *I think if I was Kerry, I'd be very nervous right now. It is a big step. And I should know... since I've got to make my mind up about it soon too, since me and Alex are heading that way. If only I felt 100 per cent sure that it is what I want to do...*

Sonja fidgeted at a rag nail under the table. *They're all wondering if Kerry's all right, if she's nervous.* Sonja winced as she tore away more skin than she meant to. *I wonder what they'd say if they knew what I'd gone through lately? I mean, I'm not pregnant – thank God – but what if I had been? What would they have thought then?*

Tapping her purple-painted nails on the glass salt cellar cradled in her hands, Cat allowed herself a little smile. *If only they knew. If only they knew what I told Kerry! They all think I'm this wild child who's had more sex than school dinners. What a joke – bang would go my reputation if they knew I was still a virgin!*

Anna finished fixing her hair and picked up her tray again. *So the girls think Kerry's going to be in a tizz about the holiday and the sleeping arrangements, do they? Well, if only they'd seen what I saw last night...*

ARE YOU A BEACH BABE?

• •

Ollie and Kerry are off to Ibiza for a romantic week of sea, sand and sunsets – they hope. It could be the holiday of a lifetime – or it could end up as a severe case of sunburn!

What kind of fun do you like to have in the sun? The holiday that makes you happiest can tell a lot about the type of person you are. Try our quiz and find out...

(1) Close your eyes and imagine you're on a beach. What three things might you be doing?

a) Smothering yourself in Factor 15, lying flat out, listening to your CD Walkman.

b) Swimming, snorkelling, getting towed behind a speedboat on an inflatable banana.

c) Paddling, giggling, eating ice-cream.

(2) What sound most reminds you of the seaside?

a) Whatever happens to be on your CD Walkman while you're sunbathing.

b) The splash of waves hitting the beach.

c) The noise of a funfair.

(3) Apart from sunscreen, what's your holiday must-have?

a) A really cool bikini – style matters, even on the sand.

b) A guide book so you can read up on all the things to see and do.

c) A nice dark pair of shades – perfect for boy-babe watching!

(4) What shoes did you pack in your suitcase?

a) Flowery flip-flops for the beach; chunky high ankle-strapped sandals for clubbing at night.

b) A pair of comfy Birkenstocks and trainers for all the walking you'll be doing.

c) Anything that won't fly off when you're spinning round on fairground rides!

(5) Uh-oh – so much for summer sun. You wake up at your holiday resort and find that the sky is full of ominously black clouds. What do you do?

a) Go straight back to bed.

b) Decide it's a day for exploring rather than sun-worshipping.

c) Break open the board games!

(6) What food do you most associate with the beach?

a) Hot dogs from beachside cafes.

b) Calamari, or whatever the local speciality is.

c) A stick of rock.

(7) What would be your ideal holiday high?

a) Getting up and dancing on a podium at the coolest club in town – preferably with a gorgeous dance partner.

b) Paragliding off a cliff – preferably with the hunkiest instructor.

c) Being at the top of a rollercoaster, just about to shoot down – preferably with a bunch of your best mates to scream along with.

(8) What souvenir would you take home with you to remind you of the good times you had?

a) A signed dance CD from the DJ at the club you went to.

b) A shell from a deserted beach you discovered when you were out exploring.

c) A six-foot cuddly toy crocodile that you won on a fairground stall.

NOW CHECK OUT HOW YOU SCORED...

SO, ARE YOU A BEACH BABE?

Mostly a
The three 'S's are important to you when it comes to holidays: sleeping, sand and sun-down. Sleeping, because you do a lot of that after a hard night's clubbing; sand, because that's what you'll be lying flat out on once you drag yourself out of bed and down to the beach; and sun-down, because for you, that's when your day really begins. Your best holiday companion would probably be Matt or Cat – you're the kind of people who need a holiday to get over your holiday!

Mostly b
Sunbathing is at the bottom of your summertime schedule, because it would bore you to pieces! You'd much rather be playing frisbee in the sand with a bunch of mates, or getting out and exploring than lying on a beach slowly barbecuing. Like Kerry, you'd hate the idea of going back home with nothing to show for your holiday than a bad case of sunburn. For you, it's a case of see and do, not just sea and sand!

Mostly c

You know how to have fun, whether your holiday's a posh villa in the Seychelles or a cramped caravan on a windy beach in Blackpool! Like Ollie, what makes a holiday perfect for you is who you're with and enjoying yourself, not where you are. You'd be just as happy crashing about on a bumper car at a seaside funfair, or picnicking in a thunderstorm – as long as you've got the right company.

Sugar

SECRETS...

...& Revenge

LOVE!
Cat's in love with the oh-so-gorgeous Matt and don't her friends know it.

HUMILIATION!
Then he's caught snogging Someone Else at Ollie's party.

REVENGE!
Watch out Matt – Cat's claws are out...

Meet the whole crowd in the first ever episode of Sugar Secrets.

Some secrets are just too good to keep to yourself!

Collins

An imprint of HarperCollins*Publishers*

www.fireandwater.com

Sugar
SECRETS...

...& Lust

DATE-DEPRIVATION!
Sonja laments the lack of fanciable blokes around, then two come along at once.

MYSTERY STRANGER!
One is seriously cute, but why is he looking for Anna?

LUST!
Will Sonja choose Kyle or Owen – or both?!

Some secrets are just too good to keep to yourself!

Collins
An imprint of HarperCollins*Publishers*

www.fireandwater.com

Sugar
SECRETS...
...& Dramas

PARTY PARTY!
Seems like everyone's having fun.
Everyone except Anna, that is...

SCHEMES!
Matt and the others are making plans –
but will their dreams come true?

DRAMAS!
Cat's really acting up again – and this
time she's having a ball!

*Some secrets are just too good to
keep to yourself!*

Collins

An imprint of HarperCollins*Publishers*

www.fireandwater.com

Order Form

To order direct from the publishers, just make a list of the titles you want and fill in the form below:

Name *TANIA Norman / 01234 841804 /*

Address *21 Viking Grove*

Kempston ~~Kempston~~

Beds MK42 8UD

Send to: Dept 6, HarperCollins Publishers Ltd, Westerhill Road, Bishopbriggs, Glasgow G64 2QT.

Please enclose a cheque or postal order to the value of the cover price, plus:

UK & BFPO: Add £1.00 for the first book, and 25p per copy for each additional book ordered.

Overseas and Eire: Add £2.95 service charge. Books will be sent by surface mail but quotes for airmail despatch will be given on request.

A 24-hour telephone ordering service is available to holders of Visa, MasterCard, Amex or Switch cards on 0141-772 2281.

Collins
An *Imprint* of HarperCollins*Publishers*